School
and
My Bully Experience

Frank Joseph Minichetti

School and My Bully Experience

The Library of Congress Cataloging-in-Publication Data has been applied for.

School and My Bully Experience is published by MinkDukane Publishing.

Date published furnished upon request.

Paperback ISBN: 978-1-7338734-0-6
eBook ISNB: 978-1-7338734-1-3

Library of Congress Control Number (LCCN): 2019908444

Cover design by 99designs.com
Interior graphic images by Peter Dmitrieff
Typesetting/Formatting by selfpublishinglab.com

Summary: Joseph Minnow is a timid thirteen-year-old that not only has to deal with bullies, but also the dreaded Sister Superior, his eighth-grade teacher. Join Joseph as he tries to survive eighth and ninth grade.

Chapters 1–16 (save for chapter 2 and portions of 14, 15, & 16) of this book are a work of fiction, loosely based on my life. Names, characters, locales and events are the product of the author's imagination. However, chapters 17–21 are non-fiction. Some information in the last six (6) chapters was obtained directly from the internet. (See End Notes for links and detailed information)

Disclaimer: For chapters 16–21, every effort was made to describe the information obtained from the internet accurately as of the publication date. Please note that companies and individuals make changes to their websites, links, subject matter and policies, so this information is subject to change. The author makes no guarantees regarding this information. You should check directly with each company/individual for the most up-to-date-information.

Acknowledgements

I would like to pay special thanks and appreciation to the persons below who provided valuable assistance and support throughout my writing of this book.

To my fabulous editor, Kim Birdsell, I can't thank you enough for your editing expertise, advice and guidance, and for always making yourself available, while answering all my questions.

I want to thank Mike Valentino (editor) for your fantastic edits and helpful suggestions.

My special thanks to Peter Dmitrieff, for your editorial comments and for creating the graphic images that helped bring the book to life.

My deepest gratitude to Sharon Bragin, for your fabulous edits.

A big thank you to Angela Levitan, for giving me a great idea for a story line.

A huge thank you to Kris Ann for your painstaking review and edits and for being the perfect daughter.

My sincere thanks to my wonderful wife, Bette, for your help and support and for being wonderful.

I also owe thanks to my best friend, Ken Uhlmann, for being my friend since high school and for teaching me how to rock and roll.

I especially want to thank Dianna Angelli for giving me the opportunity to have teachers and students critique my book.

A tremendous thank you to Christina McCann for discussing the book with her Language Arts class which generated extremely valuable feedback.

And finally, to you the reader, thank you so much for taking the time to read *School and My Bully Experience.* The greatest reward an author can receive is when someone reads their book.

"People say sticks and stones may break your bones, but names can never hurt you, but that's not true. Words can hurt. They hurt me. Things were said to me that I still haven't forgotten."
~Demi Lovato

"I allowed myself to be bullied because I was scared and didn't know how to defend myself. I was bullied until I prevented a new student from being bullied. By standing up for him, I learned to stand up for myself."
~Jackie Chan

Contents

Preface

M ost of my memories about school were happy ones; however, people who were bullies directly caused many of my bad memories.

Although I had to deal with bullies throughout my school years, my worst experiences occurred in eighth and ninth grade.

Bullying has been around since the beginning of time; however, it has now reached epidemic proportions and continues to rise.

My sincere hope is to raise awareness about this serious problem and to provide guidance regarding what can be done if you or someone you know becomes a victim.

The story opens in the present time but quickly goes back in time to the year 1965. Thirteen-year-old Joseph Minnow is good-natured, extremely timid and very trusting of everyone. Given his personality traits, Joseph soon discovers he is the perfect target for bullies. Joseph feels as if he is walking around with a sign on his back with the words, "Please Bully Me."

Joseph not only has to deal with bullies, but also the terrifying Sister Superior, his eighth grade teacher. Her voice was so loud and horrifying that the screeching of the mythical Banshee would pale in comparison.

After graduating eighth grade, Joseph soon discovers that the bullies in high school are much worse than the bullies in middle school. However, in spite of being tormented by bullies, something wonderful happens to Joseph—his first girlfriend, Katie.

Eventually, the story morphs back to the present time, when Joseph becomes a father and substitute teacher and realizes bullying has reached epidemic proportions and witnesses the latest form of bullying—the **"Cyberbully."**

Although bullying is a serious subject, *School and My Bully Experience* contains funny and entertaining stories. Finally, the book addresses some practical topics such as "Why Do People Bully?" and "What To Do If You Become a Victim." It is this combination of humorous and engaging stories, coupled with detailed information about bullying, that young readers will find both entertaining and informative, which makes School and My Bully Experience unique amongst books written on this subject.

~ Remember these words:
Never be bullied into silence. ~

1

Eighth Grade and Sister Superior

Let me take you back in time. WAIT, HOLD ON. Before we go back in time, it's important to let you know that it's been many years since I attended school, so many in fact, I can hardly remember. I'm married now and have a daughter named Emma. One day, Emma came home from middle school and she was crying hysterically. She said she was bullied at school. After she explained to me what happened, I told her I would contact the principal and straighten this out. I assured my daughter that it was going to be all right. She started to feel better. She went up to her room to call her friend, who really made her feel better. You know, it's a girl-bonding thing. After listening to my daughter, I sat down in my favorite chair. I closed my eyes and began to daydream, my mind drifted back to when I attended school. I thought about my teachers, classmates, school activities and my own personal experience with bullies. To my surprise, the memories were powerful and still intact. Join me as I reminisce about my past experiences.

Let's go back, way back, to the year 1965. It was a typical morning, nothing unusual happening. It was about 7:00, time to climb out of bed and get ready for school. I was never a morning person, so it was always a struggle for me to get going at that hour of the day. My mom was constantly telling me to "get up, it's time for school". Since I was always late, my Dad would get annoyed and say, "My boy, the ship of life is going to pass you by." I never quite understood what that meant, but he would say it often. Anyway, I proceeded to conduct my morning ritual to get ready for school… wash my face, brush my teeth, comb my hair, get dressed and eat my breakfast. When finished, I got my book bag (which looked like a miniature version of the briefcase my Dad took to work) and went off to school. We lived close to school; it was about a fifteen-minute walk. By the way, my name is Joseph Paul Minnow and I'm thirteen years old. I'm an easy-going kid, very trusting of everyone, a little timid, good-natured, just your typical average kind of guy. I have a dog named "Pudgy" and a canary, named "Perky". Little did I know, but would eventually find out due to my character traits, I was the perfect person to be bullied. It was like I had a large sign on my back with the words, **"PLEASE BULLY ME."**

Back in 1965, school was very different than it is today. There were no cell phones, Smart Boards, Facebook, Twitter, Instagram, MySpace or Snapchat. The internet was non-existent; we didn't even have computers. For each grade level, the same teacher taught all the subjects. We didn't change classrooms; we remained in the same classroom all day. Can you imagine being with the same teacher all day? It wasn't a pleasant experience.

I attended a Catholic school in a small town in North Jersey. Most of the teachers who taught there were nuns and as luck would have it the nun that taught my eighth-grade class was Sister Superior. She was called Sister Superior because she was in charge of all the other nuns. In fact, she was in charge of everything. She set school policy, decided what books we would use for each subject, made every decision regarding school activities and even planned the lunch menu. In other words, she was the boss.

Don't let the fact that she was a nun or small in stature fool you. Sister Superior was terrifying! Although she was only four foot five inches tall, her voice, personality, presence and actions made her appear to be seven feet tall. Everyone was afraid of her: teachers, parents and students, even the priests were fearful. Why? First, it was her appearance. She was dressed in a completely black habit, (except for a white head cover), black shoes, black headdress and black socks. Her eyes were dark black, like doll eyes or like the eyes you see on some stuffed animals. When she looked at you, you couldn't sense any compassion. Oh yeah, one other thing: her face sported a slight beard.

Next, her voice; it was a high pitched shrill. When she spoke she was very loud, as though she was constantly screaming. A sound so horrifying that the shrieking of the mythological Banshee would pale in comparison. She knew every school rule, not because she had a great memory, but because she was the one who created them.

We called her **"TNT"**. For the unfamiliar, TNT is a highly explosive substance.

Sister Superior

Sister Superior was a dynamo, like a nuclear bomb ready to explode at any moment. We meant no disrespect calling Sister TNT; it was said strictly out of fear. Although no one wished Sister any harm, some of us wished we could transport her into the Phantom zone like some of the criminals in the Superman comics.

One day while in class, Sister suddenly stopped teaching. She screamed out at the top of her lungs, "KAREN HAWKINS, ARE YOU WEARING MAKEUP?" Her dreadful voice filled every nook and cranny as it completely engulfed the entire room.

Karen Hawkins always sat in the last seat in the back of the class. How Sister was able to see from that distance that Karen was actually wearing makeup is still a mystery. We all just assumed Sister Superior had built in sonar and radar capabilities that were a gift from God. She told Karen to come to the front of the room. Caught off guard, the poor girl froze for an instant. After a few seconds, she got up and began to walk toward Sister. If she moved any slower she would have been walking backwards. Karen stood in front of Sister immobile and tense. After a quick examination Sister screamed out, "I knew it. You *are* wearing makeup! Young lady, go to the bathroom and wash it off immediately!" As Karen turned to leave the room, Sister Superior somehow noticed something on her lips. "Is that lip-gloss you are wearing?" Sister noticed the lip-gloss even though the color was flesh-tone. "NO, NO, NO!" She quickly added, "Make sure you wash that off as well." Needless to say, Karen never wore lip-gloss or makeup again.

Regarding the dress code, the girls had to wear the school uniform, which was a green/gray plaid skirt, white blouse and hideous saddle shoes.

As you may have guessed, the skirts had to be a certain length, which only Sister Superior seemed to know. Can you believe that she used a ruler to determine the length? If Sister thought the skirt appeared to be too short, she would measure to confirm. If short, (even by only 1/8th of an inch), Sister would send a note home to the girl's parents with instructions on how to adjust it to the proper length. It seemed like it was the school's mission to make the girls as unattractive as possible. God forbid a girl should catch the attention of a boy.

No one knew exactly why, but Sister Superior paid very close attention to the saddle shoes. For girl's that never owned a pair, the center and back portion of the shoe contained black leather while the rest was white leather. Although the shoes were iconic back in 1965, they were still ugly.

That the shoes were always polished was another of Sister's school rules. Not only must they be polished, but it was absolutely forbidden for the white polish to contaminate the black polish and vice versa. If Sister discovered white polish on the black portion of the shoe or black polish on the white portion of the shoe, the guilty person must repair the damage correctly when they returned home.

The next day in class Sister would carefully examine the shoes. If they did not pass inspection, the wearer had to stay after school for detention. So, to avoid this embarrassment, all the girls did their best to ensure their shoes were not only polished correctly, but perfectly.

As for the boys, we didn't escape embarrassment either. We had to wear a uniform as well, a white shirt, gray pants and a tie bearing the school logo. Our tie had to be tight around the shirt collar and our shirts had to be securely tucked into our pants. Unfortunately, the boys also fell victim to the keen surveillance of Sister Superior.

Occasionally without warning, she would shout out, "Everyone stop writing, all boys stand up immediately!" (if you didn't know by now, "immediately" was one of her favorite words). She then would examine each boy with the precise eye of a drill sergeant in boot camp. If your tie was slightly loose, you must fix it immediately. If your shirt was hanging out of your pants, you were asked to go outside the classroom in the hall, tuck your shirt into your pants before returning to class. I remember daydreaming in class thinking, *boy, I can't wait to go to high school where I don't have to wear a uniform.*

Another incident occurred with Skylar. She was sitting in front of Hailey. Apparently for no reason, Sister walked up to Skylar and with the force that Thor (God of Thunder) uses to wield his hammer, slammed her fist on Skylar's desk and shouted, "Stop humming, I heard you humming." Skylar with a puzzled look on her face replied, "But Sister, I wasn't humming, it was Hailey." Sister looking angrier screamed out, "Don't you *but* me young lady and never blame someone else for your own wrongdoing, just sit in silence and pay attention. Instantly, the entire class sat in complete silence. However, we all thought Sister's actions were totally unfair.

Oh yeah, I almost forgot, one of the worst mistakes you could make is to roll your eyes at Sister. Whatever you do, don't do that. If you succumbed to that gesture, Sister would be on you like white on rice. Her full reaction and punishment was so severe and scary I'm afraid to describe the details in writing. Let's just say, "Never roll your eyes at Sister."

Oh my God, I forgot something else. How could I ever forget to tell you what may be the worst thing Sister ever did to a student? It happened to Monica Wells or, should I say, Monica's hair. You see, Monica had long, flowing, beautiful blond hair, down past the center of her back.

Sister Superior noticed that Monica's hair was becoming a nuisance and a distraction. Her hair would often get into Monica's eyes or into her food at lunchtime. It would frequently get caught in her coat zipper and her hair would lay on top of the person's desk sitting behind her. At times it would cause boys to lose their concentration and focus. More importantly, though, Sister believed Monica's hair to be an outward display of pride, in turn demonstrating an utter lack of humility, which was unbecoming of a young lady.

Later that evening, Sister attended the monthly PTA (Parents Teachers Association) meeting. This is where the parents meet the teachers to discuss a student's scholastic progress and other issues. During her meeting, Sister met with Monica's parents. She told them that their daughter was very smart and a good student. However, she also expressed her concern about Monica's hair. Surprisingly, Monica's parents completely agreed with Sister and said they were trying to persuade Monica to cut her hair, but Monica always refused. Sister told Monica's parents she would take care of it.

The next day in class Sister noticed that Monica's hair was in a ponytail. This was unusual for her; she rarely wore her hair in a ponytail. Sister decided to seize the opportunity. She grabbed the scissors and with stealth-like movement and blazing speed, positioned herself behind Monica. With the skill of a surgeon using a scalpel, Sister cut off Monica's ponytail. This took Monica by complete surprise, but she was helpless to stop her. Realizing what had happened Monica jumped out of her seat and ran screaming into the girl's bathroom. The entire class looked on in horror and disbelief; we were mortified, stunned. We all wondered, did this really happen? Isn't that illegal? It was like we were having a nightmare, but we were all still awake. How could Sister do such a thing? We all thought it was cruel and heartless.

Monica was absent from school the next couple of days, but as time went on she seemed to accept her shortened locks and returned to school. Regrettably, Monica never forgave Sister and except for responding to questions in class, never spoke directly to her again.

From an early age, I always admired the nuns who taught in our school, even though we all made fun of them from time to time. They were strict and except for an occasional lack of good judgment, were also fair-minded, kind and treated each student with respect.

As a thirteen-year-old boy who normally didn't pay much attention to anything, I noticed how much they cared about us, the students. I did not always agree with their methods, but I admired them because they were totally devoted to teaching children. It seemed that in addition to their faith in God, teaching was the most important part of their life, actually their sole purpose in life.

Yes, attending Catholic school was a wonderful experience. I learned much more than the fundamentals of reading, writing and arithmetic. School taught me how to respect others and equally important, how to respect myself.

Furthermore, school taught me the rewards of hard work, the difference between right and wrong and the importance of having God as part of my life. I felt truly blessed.

In addition to Sister Superior, there were other nuns who taught in school, Kindergarten through seventh grade.

Sister Angelica taught seventh grade...

Sister Angelica was over six feet tall, but that wasn't the most unusual thing about her. She spoke very softly, so softly in fact, you could barely hear her. Her voice sounded like she was speaking to you from a far distance, when in fact, she was only a few feet away. Even a bat with highly sensitive hearing and echolocation would find hearing Sister's voice a challenge. Sister wrote much of the day's lesson on the blackboard. In 1965, the blackboards were made of black slate and we used white chalk to write on them. There were no smart boards back then. Since it was so difficult to hear Sister speak, we were all extremely happy she wrote the lesson on the board. We all suspected Sister realized she spoke softly and thought it would be best to write the lesson on the board, so we wouldn't miss anything.

Sister had this thing about being a good listener. "Class, we all need to be good listeners," said Sister. "Listening is extremely important if you want to be successful in school and later on in life. Being a good listener is essential and will make you a better person. Listening shows respect to the person speaking."

One day, James Smith began talking to his friend in class while Sister was talking. Sister would get very upset when someone spoke while she was speaking. You see, she believed this was disrespectful and made her uncomfortable because she had to speak over James. Actually, it was much more than that. Apparently, to her, this action was one of the most horrible, egregious, dreadful, disgraceful sins known to mankind. We thought it was no big deal, but apparently we were very wrong. Sister felt the same if someone spoke out of turn or failed to raise his/her hand when asking or answering a question.

As a consequence of this, Sister made James stay after school. For his punishment, he had to read a book out loud while Sister sat directly in front of him. This made him nervous and very uncomfortable. After reading for twenty-five minutes straight, which seemed like an eternity to James, Sister looked at him with an intimidating stare and asked, "So, James, how did it make you feel to read your book in front of me?"

James replied sheepishly, "Very uncomfortable."

Sister said, "Now you know how I feel when you speak when I'm talking in class. In addition to making me uncomfortable, your actions are disrespectful and annoying. I hope you learned a valuable lesson, James."

James said, "Yes, Sister. Going forward I will not talk in class while you are speaking." She then told James he could go home. He quickly shot up and left. He couldn't get out of there fast enough.

Sister Theresa taught sixth grade...

Sister Theresa always wore her hair in a bun. However, this was not your average size bun; it was enormous. All the nuns wore a headpiece that was part of their habit. Sister Theresa's headpiece looked like a rocket ship waiting to blast off. On some days it resembled a teepee that sat way on top of her head. Apparently, she had a lot of hair and it took a large hat to cover it. We often joked that one day we would see smoke signals come out from the top of Sister's head.

Her hair was not what I remembered most about her, though. You see, Sister Theresa would always repeat the point she was trying to make, at least three times. This was very annoying, even for a sixth grader. For example, she would say, "Class, today in religion we will learn how the devil tempted Jesus. Yes, we will discuss how the devil tempted Jesus. Please note we will learn how the devil tempted Jesus." Oh, she would change a few words here or there, but she still essentially repeated the same message three times. She did this each and every time she wanted to make a point. We knew she wanted us to pay attention and understand the key points of the lesson, but it was so annoying we would cringe every time she did this. I guess she thought the more times she repeated her point, the better chance we would remember it. Unfortunately, for the most part, this did not work; often we still didn't pay attention or remember the lesson.

There was another classroom lesson important to Sister. Each day she would write on the blackboard the *"Banner of the Day"*. What is the Banner of the Day? Well, typically it is a thought-provoking quote to make a specific point. You can also think of it as similar to a newspaper headline. There were days when the Banner of the Day was incorporated into that day's lesson or it was just words for you to think about or ponder.

Some of Sister's favorite banners were:

- **Every day is a fresh start!**
- **Always try your best!**
- **Words cut deeper than a knife!**
- **If you have nothing good to say, be silent!**
- **Listen to your father and mother!**
- **Learning is a privilege!**

- ❖ Helping others will bring you great joy!
- ❖ Never take life for granted!
- ❖ Try to always have a smile on your face!
- ❖ You don't always get what you wish for, but you get what you work for!

Sister was very serious about each banner. As students, we didn't quite take the Banner of the Day as seriously as Sister did, but she did her best to convince us how important it was to focus on each one, regardless.

There was one thing that bothered Sister. It was the words **"you know."** In fact, the words more than bothered her; they drove her crazy. It wasn't the words themselves per se; it was how often you would repeat them when speaking. There were a few students in my class that would say, "**you know**" before each sentence or every other sentence. For example, Johnny would say something like, "**You know**, Sister, my mom always checks my homework, **you know** my mom works as a secretary, **you know** she makes me lunch every day, and on and on. Sister would constantly remind us to be aware of this. She would say, "Please try to not say, '**you know**' repeatedly when you speak."

Unfortunately, Sister's words fell on deaf ears. The kids who repeatedly said, **"you know,"** continued to do so, so apparently no force on earth could stop them.

Sister Margaret taught fifth grade...

Naturally, we used a different textbook for each subject. All the textbooks would contain the words, "*As you know*" before describing an important point. This implied that we should somehow know the specific point mentioned in the textbook. For example, *as you know*, the temperature on Mars is minus 60 degrees Celsius or *as you know*, the Napoleonic Wars started in 1803 and ended in 1815. Most of the time, we didn't know the answer. We had no idea, so Sister Margaret would always point this out and make a joke of it. For each subject taught throughout the day, we would all laugh when we saw those three little words, "*As you know.*"

Sister was an excellent teacher; however, there was one problem: she happened to smell really bad. Let me be more specific. It wasn't Sister herself who smelled bad; instead, it was the clothes she wore. Her clothes smelled musty, like they had been hanging in a humid basement closet full of mothballs for months. On some days, her clothes smelled like rotten milk that was left out of the refrigerator too long. The two aromas (rotten milk/mothballs) permeated her clothes to the point where if she was standing next to you in class, you felt like passing out or throwing up. The smell seemed to cling to her clothes like smoke does on a smoker's wardrobe.

She kind of reminded me of the Charlie Brown character Pigpen, except instead of dirt following Sister around, it was bad odor.

There were days I wished I had a bottle of Lysol spray to help mask the awful smell. I would have paid any price to get my hands on a bottle.

The other curious thing about Sister was her list of pet peeves. She told us there are certain actions or behaviors that would really get her aggravated. She would constantly remind us of which pet peeve we violated. Sister went so far as to write the list on the blackboard in the back of the classroom. She never erased them; they remained on the blackboard as a constant reminder.

Every so often, in the middle of a lesson, Sister would abruptly stop teaching and sternly say, "Class, let's all read the pet peeves out loud." I guess she felt this would help us remember them.

Some of Sister's pet peeves were:

❖ **Coming to school unprepared**
❖ **Arriving late to school**
❖ **Staring at the window, looking outside**
❖ **Not doing your homework**
❖ **Making fun of another student**
❖ **Not dressing properly or neatly**
❖ **Speaking while someone else is talking**
❖ **Not paying attention**
❖ **Disrespecting the teacher**
❖ **Not being kind to your classmates**

Sister Gertrude taught fourth grade...

Sister Gertrude's primary reason for living was to make sure every student in her class paid attention so we could be smarter and grow up to be productive human beings and make the world a better place. We called her Gert, not to her face of course, just among us guys.

Sister would watch us like a hawk. Why, you ask? The reason was that Sister believed we should be learning something new every second while we're in class. Once we stepped into her classroom, life, as we knew it, changed. We were now in constant learning mode. We must be totally focused on our studies. We must pay strict attention to Sister at all times, storing every word spoken in our mind like a library stores books of knowledge. We must never look at the clock or stare out the window. When taking a test or quiz, Sister would watch us like a private investigator, hot on a case, making sure we were looking down at our paper and not the paper of the person next to us. God forbid we were caught attempting to cheat. Sister did not only watch us, she would travel around the room and stand over our shoulders like a human drone. She buzzed around us like a nervous bumblebee whose hive was just attacked by hungry bears. To say that Sister was quick on her feet was a gross understatement. She would roam around the room with the agility of a panther.

When there was about five minutes left in the class period, Sister would passionately ask, "Can someone tell me one important piece of information you learned today? I know there may be a number of new and exciting facts to choose from, but who can tell me just one piece of knowledge or fact that made an impression on you?"

Sister would ask this question every day. Since we all knew we had to give her an answer, we would try and jot down something we heard during class.

When class ended, Sister would say, "Now boys and girls, when you go home today, remember to tell your parents at least one important piece of information you learned during class."

Sister Agnes taught third grade…

Sister Agnes would always speak very loudly. In fact, she would shout out the lesson of the day. The tone of her voice differed from that of Sister Superior. Sister Agnes' voice was like an army Sergeant, who shouted out orders to the troops. We believed that Sister thought we were all hard of hearing. We later discovered Sister believed the louder she spoke, the more students would comprehend and better remember the lesson. She was always very serious and I remember she had the same severe stoic expression on her face every day. Although I never met a zombie in real life, if I actually met one, I imagined the expression on the zombie's face would be identical to that of Sister Agnes.

In every class, the first thing Sister would write on the board was, **Brevity is the key**. She would say enthusiastically, "Children, never write a paragraph when you could capture the same message with a sentence. Wasting words is wasting time and wasting time is wasting your life." This was pretty deep for a third grader to understand; nevertheless, Sister would say it often.

Oh yes, how could I forget? There was something else about her. She was a stickler on making sure we crossed our [t's] and dotted our [i's]. If we handed in a written assignment and failed to do this, it would infuriate her. She acted like you'd committed a mortal sin, like you tried to kill someone. We were like, really, with all of the bad things going on in the world, this gets you so upset? We never understood why this made her react this way, so we all just tried to remember to do as she asked in order to stop her from going ballistic.

There was one other thing that would upset Sister even more than failing to cross our t's and dot our i's. This was something the girls would do. They would draw little hearts over the letter i, and draw a happy face inside the letter o. It would look something like this

It is ☺kay.

For some unknown reason, drawing hearts and smiling faces would get Sister extremely upset. This action would start her percolating.

When she saw this on a girl's paper, her eyes looked like inflamed burning orbs and her cheeks would turn crimson red, her entire body would heat up like a pressure cooker until, finally, she would boil over with anger.

She would make the guilty girl stand up and embarrass her in front of the class. She would justify her actions by saying, "I was embarrassed to read it, so you should feel embarrassed as well."

However, it seemed no matter what Sister said or did, some girls couldn't help themselves. It was like some unknown force made them continue to do this, much to the disappointment and aggravation of Sister.

The repeat offenders had to stay after school. For punishment the girls had to write, "I must not draw a heart over the i or make a face inside the letter o," and draw the heart and face on each sentence. The girls had to write this phrase repeatedly on the entire front and back blackboard. Oh, but the punishment didn't stop there. After the girls completed covering both blackboards with this phrase, they had to go back and erase each heart and replace it with a period and then they had to meticulously erase the small face inside every letter o.

Sister Constance taught second grade…

Sister Constance was extremely good-natured, enthusiastic and took great pride in teaching. She told her students that she cared about each and every one of them very deeply. According to Sister, second grade was a very important grade because they were on the path to becoming young adults.

There was a very funny phrase she would often say, and it was, "**Oh, butterscotch**." When Sister would get frustrated or a little mad she would always start her response with, "**Oh, butterscotch**." For example, one day she forgot to remind us of the due date on an assignment. She said, "**Oh, butterscotch,** yesterday I forgot to tell you the assignment is due on Friday." One day, Fred was fooling around in class, Sister said, "**Oh, butterscotch,** Fred, stop it right now and pay attention."

However, there was one problem.

Sister did not treat her students like true second graders. She would treat them like they were two years old instead of second graders who were about to become young adults. The main problem was Sister would talk down to the students. Somehow, she did not realize she was doing this. This was obvious to the class because she would explain each lesson in extreme minute detail. The class felt that Sister's teaching method was an insult, even to the intelligence of a seven year old. The students all felt this way, that she was babying them. This was very annoying to everyone in class.

Sister was so annoying, students compared her to a small drip of water you hear in the middle of the night from a bathroom faucet or the high squeaking sound chalk would make while writing on the blackboard at an awkward angle.

This went on for quite some time until one day, Sister Constance was observed by Sister Superior. This was another responsibility on the long list of responsibilities of Sister Superior. She would sit in the back of the classroom and observe the teaching method and classroom skills of each teacher.

After school, Sister Constance met with Sister Superior, who explained what she was doing wrong. Sister Constance said she had no idea she was coming across that way. Sister Superior gave her a few pointers (a few pointers to Sister was actually a very long list) on how to properly speak to the students. Going forward, Sister Constance made the necessary adjustments and improved her teaching style. However, every once in a while she would forget what Sister Superior told her and go back to her old ways, much to the displeasure of the students.

Sister Madeline taught first grade...

Sister Madeline was the perfect first grade teacher. She had a warm and friendly personality and was just a very nice person who adored the children. One of the best things about Sister was she always had a smile on her face. It seems that whatever happened during class, no matter the circumstance, she would always quickly and calmly figure out the solution and say with a nonchalant tone, "No big deal. We will figure this out together."

There was one unusual thing about Sister. Her shoes squeaked when she walked. In fact, her shoes made so much noise students would compare the sound to a shopping cart with one bad wheel you get from the grocery store. When you pushed the cart, the wheel would intermittently get stuck and make a high pitch squeal sound. We never understood why she never did anything to try to stop her shoes from squeaking. It was as if she did not realize her shoes made noise. We all wondered how could she not know. Was she hard of hearing?

When Sister moved around the room and got close to a student, the students would whisper, "Here comes the shopping cart." The only good thing about this was you always knew when she was coming near you; this was especially helpful when you weren't paying attention or fooling around. Her shoes acted like an early warning signal.

Sister had three favorite sayings and she would constantly repeat the following phrases:

- ❖ **Do it with passion or not at all!**
- ❖ **Watch your habits, they become your character!**
- ❖ **Believe in the magic of life!**

Sister was always telling us to ask questions. She would say, "I don't know if you don't understand something unless you tell me, so always ask questions." Her favorite line was, "There is no such thing as a bad question."

One day Sally asked, "Why does my dog eat his poop?"

Sister said, "Congratulations, Sally, you managed to be the first person to ask a bad question." We all just laughed, even Sister.

Sister Katherine taught Kindergarten...

Sister Katherine was perfect in every way. She was like a mom to all the children. There was not one unusual or quirky thing about her. She just loved to teach and loved children. Enough said.

Oh, I just remembered, here is my picture.

Joseph Minnow

2

Positive Messages

One of my many memories of school was all of the posters and signs illustrating a variety of positive, thought provoking messages. The school labeled each message as a rule. In class, we would be reminded to read the rules because their message would make us a better person. Unfortunately, as a kid in eighth grade, I rarely paid attention to them. However, as I grew older, I had come to appreciate them much more and found the words inspiring and beneficial.

Some of the messages were just a sentence or two, while others were in a list form, like the Ten Commandments. Since I was in a Catholic school, some of the messages had religious overtones. The school created some of the messages, while others were from someone who was famous. Some of the more memorable messages from my school days are:

Classroom Rule

1. Come prepared every day to learn in class.
2. Participate in class.
3. Never give up.
4. Respect yourself, your teacher and others.
5. Pay attention.
6. Listen to your teacher.
7. Always do your best.
8. Be on time.

— Faculty

Logic Rule

Logic will get you from A to B: Imagination will take you anywhere.

— Albert Einstein

Character Rule

Be Kind	>>	But Not Weak
Be Strong	>>	But Not Rude
Be Bold	>>	But Don't Bully
Be Humble	>>	But Not Timid
Be Proud	>>	But Not Arrogant

Be Confident   >>   But Not Cocky
       — Zig Zigler

Courage Rule

1.   Have the courage to say no.
2.   Have the courage to do the right thing.
3.   Do the right thing because it is right.
4.   These are the magic keys to living your life with integrity.
       — W. Clement Stone

Spiritual Rule

With God, nothing is impossible.
       — Father Timothy

Respect Rule

You must first respect others if you want to be respected.
       — Anonymous

Diversity Rule

We as human beings must be willing to accept people who are different from ourselves.
       — Barb Jordan

Romance Rule

Follow your heart, but take your mind along with you.
       — My Mother

Inspirational Rule

How wonderful it is that nobody need wait a single moment before starting to improve the world.

— Ann Frank

Disney Rule

It is kind of fun to do the impossible.

— Walt Disney

Attitude Rule

Attitude is a little thing that makes a big difference.

— Winston Churchill

Personal Excellence Rule

The will to win, the desire to succeed, the urge to reach your full potential… these are the keys that will unlock the door to personal excellence.

— Confucius

Abe Lincoln Rule

The best way to destroy an enemy is to make him your friend.

— Abraham Lincoln

Excuse Rule

Make an effort, not an excuse.

— Faculty

See The Light Rule

All the darkness in the world can't extinguish the light of a single candle.

— St. Francis of Assisi

3

Lunchtime Experience

By now, everyone knows that Catholic school was very strict, so I couldn't wait to get a break. I distinctly remember one of my favorite periods of the day was lunch, not because the food was good, but we all got a break from going to class and doing schoolwork. We couldn't wait for lunch; but wouldn't you know it, even during lunch, school rules were strictly enforced.

Lunch monitors closely watched the lunchroom. They were mostly teachers (nuns) and their purpose was to ensure all students behaved and ate their lunch, all of their lunch, every last crumb.

The monitors would also keep a sharp eye out for anyone who was not minding their manners, was fooling around, playing with their food or acting in an undisciplined way. The moment they noticed someone behaving badly, they would spring into action with lightning fast reflexes, like a mongoose ready to pounce on a cobra, and would instantly be in the person's face. The monitors would quickly stop anyone misbehaving. They would be in front of the kid so fast it seemed they knew what he or she was going to do before they actually did it.

One of the problems I had with lunch is we couldn't choose our meal; we had to eat whatever was served that day. The other problem was most of the food tasted awful. Some items like hot dogs and grilled cheese were okay, but just about everything else tasted terrible. Take the meatloaf, for example. It was rubbery and when you tried to cut it, the meat would stick to the sides of the knife, like *spackle* would stick to a contractor's trowel. It was even difficult to scrape off with the fork.

The tomato sauce on the spaghetti with meatballs tasted burnt, like it was left cooking on the stove too long and the meatballs were hard and crusty. When you cut the meatball with your knife, it sounded like you were sawing a small piece of wood. The pizza tasted like cardboard with Italian sauce flavoring. Can you believe that even a hamburger tasted awful? It was greasy and grisly and hard to chew. We all thought, *how could you possibly mess up a hamburger?* but somehow the school had managed to do so.

Although the lunches usually tasted awful, I always tried to eat all my food (school rules); however, there were a few times I found it impossible to eat.

One day we had potato soup. I took one spoonful and it tasted yucky. It was lumpy, thick, spicy and smelled abysmal, Ughhh. I almost threw up. You see, we were constantly told if you didn't eat all of your food that it was a sin. We were reminded that children were starving all over the world, so we had to eat all our food. I never quite understood this reasoning, but it was drilled into our heads quite often, especially at lunchtime.

Anyway, getting back to my potato soup. One of the school monitors noticed I was not eating my soup. The next thing I knew the monitor was in my face insisting I eat it. I said, "I'm sorry, I tried to eat it, but it tastes awful."

The monitor called Sister Superior and when she saw I didn't eat the soup she said, "Joseph, you know the rules about food. You must eat all of it. If you don't, you must bring it to class."

Well, lunch ended and I did not eat the soup, so I brought it to class.

Of course, all of my classmates laughed at me when they saw me carry the soup into class.

Once in class, Sister Superior told me I had to finish the soup before I could go home. The dismissal bell rang; I gazed at the soup, it looked like hardened cement. I could not eat it, especially now in its hardened state, so Sister Superior kept me after school. I stared at the soup for what seemed to be an eternity until finally,

Sister Superior let me go home. Upon leaving Sister said, "I hope you learned from this experience."

I said, "Yes, Sister," even though I had no idea what I learned. All I could think of was, thank God I didn't have to eat the soup.

I do recall the happier times during lunch, too. After we finished eating, we were allowed to buy candy. I remember the candy like it was yesterday. We had a great selection to choose from, including:

- **Pop Rocks**
- **Candy Buttons on paper tape**
- **Necklace Candy**
- **Bonomo Turkish Taffy**
- **Pixy Sticks**
- **BB Bats**
- **Sugar Daddy**
- **Razzles**
- **Wax Lips**
- **Zagnut Bar**

I know that many of you reading this may not recognize most of the candy on the list, but back in '65, these were our favorites. The candy was spread out on a big table. We were like sharks and the candy was like blood in the water. We all gathered around the candy table and we couldn't wait to get all of that sugary sweetness into our mouths. It was like we were in candy heaven.

35

What a fabulous feeling, eating candy and not having a care in the world. If only I could feel this way every minute of every day, what a fantastic life it would be.

After lunch we all went to the school playground. Along with lunch and the end of the school day, going to the playground was another one of our "look forward to" times. Naturally, there were playground monitors assigned to police us to ensure we behaved ourselves. We all had a great time. The guys would play football, kickball and basketball or just run around and have fun. The girls would jump rope, play hopscotch, occasionally play basketball, but they mostly hung out with their favorite girl group and gossiped. I'm not 100 percent sure they were gossiping, but that's what all the guys thought.

One day, Fred Murkle was standing by himself in the middle of the playground. He wasn't bothering anyone, just enjoying the warm weather, minding his own business. The monitors were talking with each other, not particularly paying attention to anything.

Suddenly and seemingly out of thin air, Butch Barotti (you'll learn more about Butch later) maneuvered himself behind Fred and in the blink of an eye, pulled Fred's pants down. Unfortunately for Fred, at that exact moment almost everyone in the area was looking towards the middle of the playground and saw Fred standing there in his underwear.

Unfortunately, Fred got **PANTSED**.

Fred stood motionless, and then his body began to shake violently. Instantly, he turned red, his face displayed both

36

embarrassment and horror. For a moment, he couldn't move. He felt like he was stuck in quicksand. Finally, he regained enough composure to pull up his pants.

Everyone who saw what happened started to laugh uncontrollably. Seeing everyone laughing was too much for Fred to bear, so he ran erratically into school, crying hysterically.

When Sister Superior discovered what happened, she was overcome with rage. She screamed at Butch and the sound was deafening. She told Butch his actions were heartless, cruel and barbaric. She told him to think about how his sinful behavior really hurt Fred's feelings. Finally, Sister with the look of a Supreme Court Judge said, "Butch, tomorrow I will administer your punishment."

When the screaming finally subsided, we all wondered how Sister would punish Butch.

The next day in school, Butch found out his fate. Sister didn't waste any time. The bell rang at 8:00 a.m., punishment began at 8:05 a.m. For punishment, Butch had to spend the entire day, except for lunch, in the boy's bathroom in his underwear. Sister instructed one of the students, Phillip, to escort Butch into the boy's room. Phillip was assigned to act as Butch's guardian for the day. Butch removed his trousers and handed them to Phillip. Phillip brought the trousers to Sister, who placed them on Butch's chair in the classroom. During the course of the day, Sister told Phillip to bring the appropriate textbook and assignment to Butch. Since there was no chair in the boy's bathroom, Butch had no choice; he had to sit on the commode to complete each assignment. Surprisingly, mean-spirited, rough and tough Butch actually felt embarrassed. You must know by now, with Sister, the embarrassment would not end quickly. To further the embarrassment, Butch had to write a note to his parents explaining why he had to spend the entire school day in the boy's bathroom. Remember, as a rule, Sister's punishment was designed to fit the crime.

Another example of her punishment rule occurred when Adam Tucker got angry with one of the guys and swore at him. I don't remember the bad word spoken, but it really doesn't matter. Just know it was bad and it was extremely offensive to Sister. For punishment, she took some masking tape, walked slowly towards Adam and forcefully affixed the tape over his mouth. She did so with the precision of a licensed plumber using construction tape to cover a leaky pipe.

Sister instructed Adam not to remove the tape until she could determine the appropriate time required to satisfy the punishment. Using divine intervention, Sister's heavenly influenced decision was that the tape could be removed in exactly thirty-nine minutes. Don't ask why the time had to be exactly thirty-nine minutes. Remember, it was determined via divine intervention.

Sister looked at Adam and with a cold blank stare said, "Breathe through your nose. I will tell you when to remove the tape. In the meantime, think hard about how you will avoid using vulgar language and speak with dignity as you move forward with your life."

After the thirty-nine minutes had passed, Sister told Adam to remove the tape. Adam was allowed to speak freely; however, Sister reminded Adam that from now on he must choose his words more carefully.

4

Back in the Classroom

After lunch we returned to class. Once in class, we often got into trouble, like the time a group of us went into the boy's bathroom. There I was with my friends in the boy's room, we were all fooling around and acting stupid. We were wetting paper towels and tossing them up onto the ceiling. The paper towels would stick to the ceiling and we all thought it was hilarious. We believed we were safe from Sister Superior; we thought there was no way she would come into the boy's bathroom. Little did we know that Simon Brown (the teacher's favorite), who never did anything wrong in his entire life, squealed on us. He told Sister

Superior we were fooling around. Faster than humanly possible, Sister came running into the bathroom (she would have beat The Flash or Superman in a race that day). She looked up at the ceiling and in what turned out to be an unbelievable moment of bad luck, one of the paper towels fell down and hit her square in the face. Well, Sister went berserk. She started screaming, "Everyone out and back to class at once!"

On the way back to class, we all started to worry about what Sister was going to do to us, except for Butch Barotti, who never seemed to worry about anything. When back in class, Sister told each of us to come to the front of the classroom and line up. In a serious and unforgiving voice she said, "Hold out your hands." Sister grabbed her pointer, the one she used to point out the states on the map of the United States, and proceeded to walk very slowly to the first boy in line. She said, "What I'm about to do is going to hurt me more than it hurts you." We all thought *I doubt that.* The next thing we heard was **"WHACK,"** as she hit the hand of the first boy. Sister would always try to punish the part of the body responsible for the wrongdoing. This may come as a big surprise, but back when I was in school the nuns were permitted to hit you. The next guy in line really got nervous because he knew he was the next one to get hit. Sister hit each of us. She wasn't bashful when she hit us. She used extreme force and it really hurt. When our punishment was complete, she told us to return to our seats and said, "I hope you learned your lesson."

At that moment I thought Sister would fit right in during the Middle Ages in Rome, where the Roman guards would whip prisoners. I realized something else. No matter how often we got punished, there were always some people who would never learn their lesson.

The next day we were all back in the classroom. I was sitting in my seat, not paying attention, looking out the window. The next thing that happened took me by complete surprise. Sister threw an eraser at me and with the accuracy of a Major League pitcher, hit me square on the side of my head. I had thick black hair and the eraser left a white patch of chalk where it hit me. My friend sitting next to me told me my hair was covered in white chalk. I began to wipe it off when Sister shouted, "No, do not wipe it off until the end of class. Maybe the chalk will serve as a reminder to always pay attention in class."

There was another unfortunate event that happened, we had to take a test. To make matters worse, it was a math test. Boy, do I hate math tests. It seemed like as much as I hated taking tests, Sister loved to administer them.

Then, Sister did something curious.

Before distributing the test, Sister went around the room and handed each student a pencil and scissors. We all had a puzzled look on our faces. Why did Sister give us scissors? This was a math test, nothing to do with arts and crafts. It didn't take long for us to find out. Sister said, "Boys and girls, there is a reason I gave you scissors. Please listen to my instructions carefully. I want the class

42

to do the next task together, at the same time. Ready, pick up the pencil and using the scissors, snip off the eraser. Be careful to cut the end of the eraser as close as possible to the metal casing and make sure the eraser does not fall on the floor. I will be coming around to pick it up. The reason we are doing this is that I do not want you to erase your answers. Instead, you should carefully think of the answer before recording it. It is extremely important to get the answer correct the first time. There are too many instances where I see students rush their answer, make careless mistakes, then erase and correct it. These mistakes can be avoided if you just take the time to carefully think before you write." Sister became silent, then said, "Remember, **haste makes waste**."

We all looked at each other. Somehow, I sensed we were all thinking the same thing, *sister never ceases to amaze*.

Oh, there was one more surprise. Sister told us to carefully follow the test instructions. The instructions stated to complete only problems one through ten. Sister instructed us to begin. I started to record my answers. I soon realized that some of my classmates quickly finished the test. I thought to myself, *how is this possible, how can they be done so fast?* I was the last one to hand in my test.

Sister then read the instructions, which stated to only complete the first ten questions out of the thirty. All of a sudden it hit me. I completed all thirty questions, but only had to complete ten. I felt awful. Sister taught us a valuable lesson, always read and carefully follow instructions. From that day on, I always carefully followed instructions.

5

My First Bully Experience

In school, we were all afraid of this one boy. His name was BUTCH BAROTTI. Butch was the biggest boy in the eighth grade and looked much older than his actual age. He looked like he could play middle linebacker for the New York Giants. His father made him get a buzz cut (except for a few sprigs of hair standing straight up on the top of his head). He also wore a gold earring. He looked like a Marine in basic training. Butch had a mean disposition and he seemed angry all the time.

Butch took great pleasure in intimidating people and making you feel uncomfortable. At home, even his dog did not escape his bully antics. He would offer his dog food, but never let him eat it. He would grab the dog by the neck and choke it. He would constantly antagonize his dog. The dog was not the only animal he tortured. What he did to his cat was even worse. He would grab the cat and throw it into the toilet bowl and attempt to flush it down the toilet. Fortunately, the cat was too big to actually get sucked down into the toilet. Butch wasn't satisfied with only one flush; he would flush the toilet multiple times before letting the cat out. When Butch opened the lid, the cat would bolt out like a flash of lightning. Afterwards, when the cat saw Butch walking around the house, it would always run in the opposite direction.

This should give you a pretty good idea of the kind of person he was. This type of behavior screams out **"I'm a Bully!"**

Butch Barotti

45

Before class, I was speaking with one of my friends (Theo) about Butch. Theo said, "Butch is not dipping with both oars." I stared at Theo with a puzzled look on my face.

Theo said, "You know, the lights are on, but nobody's home."

It suddenly hit me," Oh, you mean he's a little crazy."

Theo nodded. "Yes."

Now that you know more about Butch, let's get back to the classroom. For some reason, some boys would make fun of this one girl, Tracy Hall. She was super quiet and was kind of a loner. She was very smart, studied hard and never got into any trouble. Unfortunately, Tracy did not have any friends. At lunch, she would mostly sit by herself.

Apparently, Butch Barotti did not like her and always made fun of her. There was really no good reason for Butch not to like her, but it seems that if you're a bully you do not need a reason.

Later I would learn that Butch always tried to justify his actions by making up some story as to why he would pick on someone; or should I say, "bully" someone. In Tracy's case, the only thing Butch could pick on was Tracy's frizzy hair. It was not really frizzy, Butch just made it up. So, Butch always teased her about her hair, which made Tracy very uncomfortable and really hurt her feelings.

One day after school, a group of boys followed Tracy home.

Tracy's house was in the same direction as my house. Unfortunately for me, that day I walked home with the other boys. It was winter and there was snow on the ground. Butch and a few of the guys started to call Tracy names and began throwing snowballs at her. Tracy ran home crying. We saw Tracy's mother open the door to let her in.

The next day at school, Butch, myself and the other guys were called into Sister Superior's office. We were all afraid because we thought Sister found out what happened with Tracy. Sister always seemed to find out when we did something wrong. Apparently, Tracy told her mother we were calling her names and throwing snowballs. Tracy's mother called the school and told Sister Superior what happened. Panic stricken, immediately I told Sister I didn't call Tracy names or throw any snowballs; however, it made no difference, it turns out I was guilty by association.

Sister Superior was livid. She started screaming about our bad behavior. The color of her face morphed into a deep reddish hue, even the tips of her ears turned red. Her eyes looked like oversized ping pong balls that were about to pop out of her head, as if someone was choking her to death. She said we were disrespectful, mean-spirited and on and on she went. She yelled at us for what seemed like hours. By the time she was done, you would have thought we committed first-degree murder. When the yelling finally stopped, only one word stuck in my mind. Sister Superior called us **"BULLIES."** I distinctly remember that word **BULLY**; something sounded so ominous about that word. I know I encountered other instances of bullying in my earlier grades, but this is the first time I'd been associated with bullies or heard the word directed at me.

Of course, there was punishment. Sister made all the boys involved turn our desks around and face the back of the classroom.

If that wasn't bad enough, we then had to write the entire religion book cover to cover. Sister wasn't done, there was more. She contacted our parents and told them what had happened.

Later when I got home, I explained to my parents that I didn't call Tracy names or throw snowballs, but somehow that didn't matter. My father said, "Your mother and I agree with Sister. You were with the other boys and you must suffer the consequences."

So, I received my second punishment. I could not watch television for a week.

Things quieted down for a while. I guess we were all scared about what had happened with Tracy.

About a month later, Butch was at it again. This time he started to bully people for money. His plan was to target kids walking to and from school. He would sneak up behind you trying to catch you off guard. He then started screaming at you. After scaring you half to death, he would get right in your face and demand money, twenty-five cents to be exact.

He said he needed the money to buy candy. I know twenty-five cents seems like very little money today, but in 1965, you could buy a lot of candy with it. Butch would continue to bully people this way. Nobody said a word to Sister or his or her parents because we were all afraid that Butch would find out and try to hurt us.

Next, something happened that amazed and shocked me.

For the very first time, I witnessed a girl bully another girl.

It involved Katie Smith. Katie was one of the prettiest girls in school. Although she was pretty, she wasn't conceited and was very quiet and shy. Some of the girls in class were jealous of Katie because of her good looks.

I remember that out of all the girls in class, Beth Johnson would bully Katie the most. Since there was nothing obviously wrong or different about Katie, Beth would spread lies and rumors about her. Beth told the other girls in her circle of friends that Katie's father lost his job and that Katie was very poor and didn't have enough money to buy lunch. Beth also said the only reason Katie is smart is that her uncle is a teacher and tutors Katie every day after school, so that's the only reason she gets good grades. Beth kept saying this over and over, "The only reason Katie does well in school is because she has a tutor."

Oh, I just remembered. Since Beth talked so much, Beth's father would often say to Beth's girlfriends, "You know girls, Beth's tongue was born two weeks before she was born. The girls just laughed. Anyway, back to the story.

Beth's verbal abuse against Katie went on for weeks and weeks. Finally, one day Beth and her friends saw Katie walking home from school. Beth ran up to Katie and began teasing her again. This time she started to call her names, cruel and vicious names, names that were so bad I can't even repeat them. Then, the unthinkable happened. Katie, this sweet, quiet, nice girl turned into a ruthless, scary fighting machine.

To the amazement of Beth's friends, Katie was like the Tasmanian devil from the old Bugs Bunny cartoon; she was spinning, hitting, huffing and puffing. Beth's girlfriends watched in utter shock. They

49

couldn't believe their eyes. For a moment they couldn't breathe, their bodies were petrified with fear. Who would have ever thought this calm and gentle girl could react like this? Katie acted like a wild animal. This took Beth by complete surprise. Beth's girlfriends then witnessed something they never ever expected to see. Beth, this seemingly invincible, bossy, all-powerful, afraid of nothing girl, started to cry. Beth had no idea what hit her; she had no defense against Katie. She did the only thing she could do—run away and run away fast.

After that day, Beth never again spoke to Katie. However, all of Beth's friends who never spoke to Katie before began to talk to her. Another remarkable thing happened; Beth's girlfriends were no longer in awe of Beth. Instead of spending all their time with Beth, one by one they were spending very little time with her. They all seemed to realize maybe Beth didn't know everything and her opinion, especially about people, is greatly flawed. They all began to think more on their own and found themselves less influenced by what Beth said or did. It seemed that Beth's girlfriends learned a valuable lesson; unfortunately, the same could not be said for some of my other classmates, especially Butch and his gang of friends, which you will soon find out.

One day in school, Sister Superior made the following announcement:

"Children, I have great news. Today is a special day."

This really got us all very excited. What could Sister be talking about? There we were, sitting in class at the edge of our seats anticipating her next words. She then said excitedly, "Today you will all receive an eighth grade class ring." Sister did not stop there. Sister being Sister went on to educate us on the significance of the class ring. She said, "The class ring is very important. The ring is to commemorate your graduation from middle school. The ring makes a statement for all who look at it, that through hard work and determination you can achieve anything; in this case, graduation from eighth grade. It signifies you are ready to move on to higher education where you can continue to achieve great things."

We were all thinking, "Wow, does this little ring really mean all those things?" Sister continued and explained the history behind the class ring. She said, "The tradition of wearing class rings began in the year 1835, at the United States Military Academy at West Point. This is the school where students learn to be soldiers. The students at West Point were the first to wear a class ring. Many soldiers died in battle wearing their class ring. The soldier's ring is similar to the class ring you will receive. Just like at West Point, our school ring exemplifies our school pride and unity among students."

After school, I heard Butch talking with his friends about the ring. His voice dropping to a whisper said, "This ring is really cool and it makes us really cool. All the other kids in school will now look up to us more than ever. So guys, to be certain we have their respect, we must get the 7th grade boys to kiss our rings." For some reason the guys in his little gang thought this was a great idea, so they began to plan exactly how they were going to force the 7th graders to kiss their rings. Butch being Butch concocted a devilish plan. Each day Butch and his buddies would follow a different 7th grade boy walking home after school. When he or a group of his friends caught up with the boy, they would gang tackle him to the ground. Once on the ground they would not let him get up until he kissed their rings. Butch's friends thought this was a brilliant idea.

The next day after school, Butch and his henchmen followed Jimmy Cahill home. Jimmy soon realized that Butch and his friends were chasing after him, so he started to run. Finally, Butch caught up with Jimmy and tackled him to the ground. Butch held Jimmy down until the other guys arrived. One guy held his arms while the other guy held his feet. Next, they forced Jimmy to kiss Butch's ring. The boys switched places, holding down Jimmy until he kissed each boy's ring. Finally, they let Jimmy up; he started crying and ran home. When Jimmy got home his mother saw he was very upset and asked him what happened. Jimmy was too ashamed to tell his mother what really happened and made up some other story. His mother believed him and Jimmy went to his room.

Butch and his gang of friends continued to do this to other boys. Finally, one boy told his mother and she called the school. When Sister found out, she was overcome with rage and disappointment. She punished the boys, hoping it would stop them from bullying people in the future. You might think by now Butch learned his lesson. As it turned out, Butch and his friends not only didn't learn their lesson, they were just getting started with bullying people. There was this one girl in school, Allison, who would get sick to her stomach when she felt pressured or when someone got her extremely upset. One day she forgot to bring her homework to school. When Sister Superior found out, she asked Allison why she didn't have her homework.

Allison drew a deep sharp breath and replied, "I just forgot it." This seemed like a perfectly good answer to me, but apparently not good enough for Sister. Sister, as usual, overreacted and started yelling at her, saying she was irresponsible and being irresponsible can lead to other bad habits. Sister's voice got louder and louder as her verbal barrage continued. Finally, Allison couldn't take it anymore. Overcome with emotion, her entire body began to quiver and shake; **SUDDENLY**, she started to vomit. She threw up all over her desk, clothes and the floor. The smell was awful; it was like tuna fish when you first open the can or when your mom makes egg salad. **Whew!**

Sister told Allison to go to the girl's bathroom to clean up. She asked another girl to go help her.

Sister contacted the janitor, who cleaned up the mess. The janitor sprayed the area with a cleaning solution that smelled like mint, but unfortunately the smell made you nauseous.

After seeing what happened, Butch developed a hideous thought: *It would be fun to make Allison throw up again.* As fate would have it, Butch discovered Allison was getting new glasses after school. Butch thought he could upset Allison by making fun of her glasses. Allison was now vulnerable and Butch was ready to seize the opportunity.

The next day, Allison came to school with her new glasses. All the students were lined up outside of school waiting for the bell to ring. Butch was ready to pounce into action. When Butch saw Allison, he began to bully her. The first thing he said was, "Hey, four eyes." He didn't stop there. He said her glasses made her look ugly. He continued to bully her. He said her glasses were way to big for her face and made her head look big.

Butch's comments really hurt Allison's feelings and she started to get teary-eyed. (Butch seemed to have a special talent to know how to deeply upset people). Butch was relentless with his verbal abuse and he continued to abuse her all day. He made fun of Allison at lunch, in the playground, hallways and even in the classroom when Sister wasn't looking.

Finally, while on the playground, Allison couldn't take it anymore. Her throat began to stiffen, like you feel when you are about to cry. She started to gag and felt woozy and nauseous like she was seasick, same as the time she got sick on her uncle's boat. Powerless to stop herself, she began to vomit violently. She looked like a volcano erupting, but instead of lava, she began spewing vomit everywhere. It was disgusting. Allison wanted to crawl under a rock; she was so ashamed.

Sister Superior contacted Allison's parents. Her mother came to school and picked her up.

The next day, Allison told her mother she didn't feel well. She said she did not want to go to school. Her mother said it was okay to stay home and rest. The next day Allison told her mother she felt better, but was afraid to go to school. Her mother asked her why.

Allison said she was being bullied by one of her classmates. Her mother asked, "Who is the person bullying you."

Immediately Allison said, "I can't tell you. I don't want to be a tattletale."

Her mother said, "In this case, no one will accuse you of being a tattletale, because you are being bullied. We must put a stop to this or it will continue. Furthermore, by speaking up you may prevent someone else from being bullied."

Allison understood what her mother was saying, but still refused to tell her the bully's name. She was just too afraid of retaliation. She returned to school the next day, hoping that Butch would stop bullying her.

Regrettably, Butch continued to bully Allison for a long time. Allison just put up with it, said nothing and was often very sad, upset and sick to her stomach.

Eventually Butch moved on to bully someone else; however, not before causing Allison much pain and suffering.

It's a shame Allison couldn't find the courage to speak up. I know it's difficult, especially for me, but it's something we must all strive to do—say something.

One Saturday, a few of my friends came to my house to trade comic books. My friends and I really like to read comics and occasionally we would trade with each other. We enjoyed reading superhero comics. Our favorites were—

❖ Superman

❖ Batman

❖ The Flash

❖ Green Lantern

❖ Spiderman

❖ Legion of Super Heroes

❖ Hawkman

❖ Jimmy Olsen

❖ Dr. Strange

❖ Justice League of America

❖ Wonder Woman

We were all in my room looking at comics when my mom peeked her head in and said, "Joseph, you have another friend who wants to trade comics."

I was thinking, *all my friends who trade comics are already here.* Then, Butch, who was standing behind my mother, entered the room. I looked in horror as Butch came into my room. I closed my eyes for a moment; I thought I was having a bad dream. I was so infuriated that I clenched my fists with such extreme force I could hear my knuckles crack. I didn't want him to stay, but I didn't know how to get rid of him, so he joined us. This would turn out to be a big mistake.

We all noticed something different about Butch that day. He seemed to be friendlier, more polite. I said, "Butch, I didn't know you liked to read comic books."

"Oh, yeah," Butch said. "I love to read comics. I brought some with me to trade." We all looked at each other in disbelief. Is this really happening? Butch, the biggest bully in the school acting like a normal kid. He actually likes comics the same as we do.

The rest of the day went well. We had comics spread out all over my room. We all traded some comics, except for Butch. Curiously, Butch said he did not find any comics he wanted. We were surprised because there were a lot of comics from which to choose. Anyway, it was getting late and everyone went home.

That night, I noticed some of my comics were missing. When I told my mom, she said they must be somewhere in my room and I must have misplaced them. I began scouring the place. I looked everywhere. I knew exactly how many comic books I had and where I kept them. After completing my search, I was sure some were missing.

On Monday, while in class, I noticed Zack had two of the comics I was missing. I asked him where he got them. He said with a grin, "I bought them from Butch." At that moment it hit me; Butch stole my comic books. I thought, *no wonder Butch was so nice at my house. He had an ulterior motive.*

Butch was acting friendly and nice because he wanted to catch us off guard so he could steal comic books. He acted like one of those porch pirates. You know, the people that steal packages a deliveryman leaves on your porch or doorstep. How low can a person get? I was so mad that Butch actually stole from me. This was a new low, even for someone like Butch. I became even more angry with myself for being so trusting, allowing him to take advantage of me. It's a terrible feeling when you realize someone took advantage of you.

I told my mother what happened. She asked if I was absolutely certain Butch stole my comics. I replied assuredly, "Yes, Mom. I'm absolutely certain."

My mom believed me because she knew how careful I was with my comics and that I could be trusted.

My mother called Butch's mom and told her what happened. Initially, Butch told his mother he didn't steal the comics. However, later she noticed Butch had extra money lying on his desk. When she confronted Butch, he admitted he stole the comics.

Butch's mom was very upset that Butch would do such a thing and forced him to buy new comics to replace the ones he stole. Later, Butch and his mom came over my house and she made him apologize. He handed me the comics and said he was sorry. His mom told us she was sorry for her son's bad behavior and said Butch would be punished. Later that night, I heard my mom talking to my dad, explaining what had happened. Mom said, "I know Butch's parents and they are two of the nicest people I've ever met. How could their son be so bad? It doesn't make any sense."

I thought it might not make any sense, but it is what it is.

Butch was not only a bully, but a thief as well. Apparently, in some cases, being a bully can lead to criminal activity.

Well, we were back in class again. One of my friends from school was Laura, one of the nicest girls in school. She was very friendly and everyone liked her. Although you wouldn't know it when first meeting her, Laura was the nervous type. Scratch that, she was the extremely nervous type. The littlest thing made her jittery. Laura's personality was similar to that of Allison. Anxiety and a case of the jitters are bad traits for anyone who is a student in a class taught by Sister Superior.

Moreover, there was one thing that made Laura sad. She was self-conscious about her skin, as she had a very bad complexion.

One day in class, each of us had to stand up and read a chapter from our English book. Sister would ask questions to determine what we could remember. It was a part of reading and comprehension. When Laura finished her turn of reading, Sister began to ask her questions. Laura answered the first question. However, she struggled to answer the second. The third question, she didn't know the answer to and started to get nervous. Sister continued to rapidly fire off questions. The more questions Laura couldn't answer, the more distraught she became. Suddenly, her teeth began to chatter uncontrollably, making a sound similar to one of those novelty wind-up chattering teeth. Her body began to rattle and shake from side to side, like a washing machine that went off-kilter. She had trouble catching her breath. Sister noticed Laura was getting extremely flustered. Instead of feeling sorry for her, Sister said with a stern and aggravated voice, "Laura, I see you are getting nervous and struggling to answer the questions, but this exercise is for your own good. You must get over your nervousness. You cannot go through life acting this way."

By this time, the entire class felt sorry for Laura and we all began to grow increasingly uncomfortable as we watched her struggle to answer questions. Sister was relentless and as she furiously continued to fire off one question after another, Laura became more and more nervous, until finally, she could no longer respond. For a moment she stood motionless, as if time stood still.

Then, something terrible happened.

Laura started to pee uncontrollably. It sprayed all over her desk, clothes and the floor.

It looked like a small tsunami suddenly appeared.

We all looked on in horror as we witnessed what had happened. Laura burst into tears; she was an emotional mess. Sister Superior, showing little remorse, asked some of the other girls to take her to the bathroom. In the meantime, Sister called Laura's parents, who picked her up and took her home. Sister called the janitor, who came quickly to clean up. He sprayed the area with that green liquid, like the one used when Allison threw up. Again, the liquid smelled like fermented mint. The stench was nauseating.

Butch and his friends realized that when Laura became extremely nervous, the results could be catastrophic. In their cruel way of thinking, they began to formulate ideas of how to upset her similar to the way they antagonized Allison. It didn't take long to come up with a devious plot. Butch remembered Laura being extremely sensitive about her complexion. She had terrible acne covering much of her face and neck. Butch and his friends knew just what to do. They would all make fun of her bad skin. Butch carefully coordinated a cruel plan of attack. When the opportunity presented itself, Butch and his bully friends would all tease her unmercifully.

One day during lunch, Butch and his friends began to make fun of Laura. When the lunch monitors were not looking, they would call her names, terrible names, names that would embarrass her. They called her pizza face, crater face, pimple face, acne head, guacamole face and on and on. The comments were cuttingly insensitive and cruel. Butch and his friends would make fun of her every chance they could. They bullied her for weeks on end. Finally, one day in the hallway, Butch forced her against the wall, stepped up close to her face and repeatedly called her every cruel name he could think of. He then said, "Laura, you are even uglier close up. Your face is so ugly no one wants to be your friend. You're going to be lonely all your life. You make me sick just looking at you."

This was the final straw. Laura could not take such verbal abuse any longer. All of a sudden, she began to pee all over the floor. It just happened. She couldn't control herself. It sounded like Niagara Falls on a rainy day. Okay, maybe it wasn't that loud, but you get my point. Butch, seeing what happened, immediately began laughing and ran into the classroom.

Laura continued to stand, stiff against the wall, frozen with shame. It looked like she was glued to the wall. As time passed, it seemed like someone would have to peel her off the wall like old scotch tape. After a while, one of the teachers saw her, knew something was wrong and brought her to the office. The janitor was summoned to clean the floor, with, you guessed it, that horrible smelling green liquid. The school contacted her parents and her mom brought a change of clothes to school.

Back in class, Butch bragged to his friends that he got Laura so upset she peed on the floor. When Sister Superior realized Butch was responsible for upsetting Laura, she yelled angrily, "What you did was shameful and disgraceful." Sister hollered louder than usual. She again punished Butch. He had to serve another two-day school suspension. Sister made him apologize to Laura, which he did only because he was forced to do so. I thought to myself, *how could Butch be so thoughtless and insensitive?*

One of the smartest students in school was Preston White. One of the laziest students was Cosmo Rendone. Cosmo told everyone who would listen that he hated to do homework.

Before school started, while waiting for the first bell to ring, Cosmo came up to me and said, "Joseph, I really hate doing homework. It's boring and it takes me away from reading comic books and watching TV."

I said, "I don't like to do homework either, but it's just something we have to do. My mom told me there are things in life we don't like to do, but we have to do them because it's the right thing to do."

Cosmo had this bewildered look on his face, like what kind of nonsense are you telling me. Cosmo appeared to be annoyed by my comment and walked away shaking his head.

Cosmo thought about his dilemma for a while and finally came up with the solution. Regrettably, it was a bad solution. He decided he would force someone to give him their homework so he could copy it.

We were on the playground when Cosmo approached Preston. Cosmo said, "Hey, Preston, I need to copy your homework."

Without hesitation, Preston replied emphatically, "No. Absolutely not." Preston's refusal angered Cosmo and he became extremely agitated. He now began to threaten Preston. He said with an angry tone, "Preston, I tried to ask you nicely, but now you give me no choice. If you don't let me copy your homework, I'm going to beat you to a pulp. To show you I mean business, let me give you a sample of what to expect."

Cosmo then pushed Preston up against the fence. He pushed him so hard, the force of his body against the fence really hurt Preston. As Cosmo released Preston from his grip, he said with a menacing stare, "The next time I won't be so gentle. You will see blood, your blood. So listen up, because this is what is going to happen. You are going to meet me in the playground every morning fifteen minutes before school starts." Preston understood what Cosmo meant and walked away.

When Preston got home from school, he told his mom from now on he wants to go to school earlier than usual. His mom asked why. Preston said, "I'm going to meet my friends. We play football and basketball for a few minutes before school starts. The activity relaxes us for the long school day ahead."

Preston's mom said with a concerned voice, "Okay, but remember, this means you must get up at least fifteen minutes earlier." At that moment, Preston realized something. This was the first time he lied to his mother. Apparently, this is another bad by-product of being bullied; it sometimes leads to lying to your parents and others.

That Monday morning Preston got up early and went to school. When he arrived, he saw Cosmo waiting for him.

Reluctantly, Preston gave Cosmo his homework for Monday's class and Cosmo copied it.

Once in the classroom, Cosmo gave the homework to Sister Superior. Sister had no idea it was really Preston's work and not Cosmo's.

This routine went on for weeks and was working perfectly until one day Cosmo made a crucial mistake.

It was Friday and Cosmo arrived with only five minutes left until the bell rings. Frantically, he began to copy Preston's homework. He was under so much pressure due to time constraints, he inadvertently wrote Preston's name at the top of the page. Realizing what he had done, Cosmo quickly erased Preston's name and wrote his own name. When walking into school, Cosmo thought, *thank God I erased Preston's name and replaced it with my name. Otherwise, I would be in big trouble.*

When Cosmo arrived in class he handed his homework to Sister as usual.

After school, Sister began to review each student's homework. When she looked at Cosmo's homework she noticed the faint remains of someone else's name. After careful examination, Sister determined the name was Preston White. When Sister would notice something that looked suspicious, she'd leap into action. In this case, her actions were like a bloodhound that uses only a faint scent to track down their prey. Remember, nothing gets past Sister Superior; she notices everything.

Next, Sister compared Cosmo's homework against Preston's. Discovering they both made the exact same mistakes, she quickly realized that Cosmo copied Preston's homework. Rage and disappointment simultaneously raced through her body and soul. Copying someone else's homework is cheating and cheating was one of Sister's deadly sins. Officially, there are seven deadly sins; however, Sister had her own list.

The next day in class, Sister spoke to both Preston and Cosmo and they confessed. It didn't take Sister long to discover the truth. She used interrogation tactics that would make any police detective proud.

For punishment, Preston received a one-day detention for failing to tell anyone about Cosmo's bully behavior and Cosmo received a more serious sentence, a three-day detention for cheating and for bullying Preston.

6

Incident at Gym: The Race

As previously mentioned, lunch was my favorite time of the day. Gym was my second favorite. Mr. Robinson taught the boy's gym class. He was a lay teacher, meaning he was not a priest, just your typical teacher. Mr. Robinson was a happy go-lucky-guy, athletic, full of energy, very nice and liked by all. Every few weeks, Mr. Robinson planned a new activity for our class. He told us he never wanted us to get bored during gym class. He had a favorite saying. He said, "Boys, I know you heard the saying cleanliness is next to godliness, but I believe exercise is next to godliness. Exercise keeps your body sharp, in the same way classwork keeps your mind sharp."

During the school year, some of the activities we participated in were –

- ❖ **Basketball**
- ❖ **Whiffle Ball**
- ❖ **Touch Football**
- ❖ **Gymnastics**
- ❖ **Volleyball**
- ❖ **Dodge Ball**
- ❖ **Rope Climbing**

There were other games, but I can't remember them.

Unfortunately, Butch and his friends realized gym class presented the perfect opportunity to bully people. This is something I noticed about people who are bullies; they look for locations where it is easier to bully someone, where there are fewer or no adults present. Gym is one of those locations because during class only one teacher is present, Mr. Robinson. Furthermore, because of the nature of the games played, Mr. Robinson was often distracted.

I also realized that bullies often target transitional areas such as —

- ❖ **Hallways**
- ❖ **Playgrounds**

❖ **Cafeteria**

❖ **School Bus**

Now, let's get back to gym class.

Mr. Robinson selected teams to play basketball. At a time when I believe Mr. Robinson experienced a severe lapse in judgment, he inexplicably selected Butch and some of his friends to play on the same team. This turned out to be a huge mistake. It was the shirts against the skins. Butch was on the skins team.

We started to play.

It didn't take long before someone was bullied. Steve, who played on the shirts team, attempted a shot, and while in the act of shooting, Butch jumped on top of him and Steve fell hard to the floor. Mr. Robinson saw this and yelled, "Butch, you're playing too rough."

Butch replied indignantly, "I was just trying to block the shot." We all knew Butch was lying. We all know the difference between playing hard and trying to hurt someone. Butch's only intent was to smash Steve to the floor.

As we continued to play, there were other incidents of bullying.

My friend Jeff was driving to the basket for a layup when Zack slammed him into the post under the basket. Inexplicably, somehow, Mr. Robinson didn't see this happen. Jeff complained that Zack pushed him hard and hurt his shoulder. Instead of apologizing or feeling bad for his actions, Zack made fun of Jeff by calling him a big baby, saying he hardly touched him. This often happened. Zack, as with other bullies, would bully someone and there would be no consequences for their bad behavior.

A few weeks later, we were playing a new game, **"Whiffle Ball."** I thought by playing Whiffle Ball, my friends and I would be safe from being bullied.

I was wrong.

One of Butch's friends was pitching and I was at bat. I got a base hit, a double and began running to first base. When I rounded first, Butch, who was playing defense at first, shouted, "Joseph, that was a lucky hit you jerk!" Then he spit in my face.

This time, Mr. Robinson saw what happened. He yelled, "Butch, stop playing and go see Sister Superior this instant." Sister Superior was furious and told Butch to stay after school for detention. You would think Butch would finally learn his lesson; however, you will soon find out he didn't learn his lesson at all.

At the end of gym class, Mr. Robinson said he had a special announcement. We all couldn't wait to hear about it.

Just before the bell rang, Mr. Robinson said excitedly, "Okay, boys, are you ready to hear my special announcement?"

We were very excited and responded in unison with a **l-o-u-d**, **"YES!"**

"Okay, here goes. There will be an eighth-grade race. The winner of the race will earn the title –

"The Fastest Boy in School"

Mr. Robinson continued to explain the details of the race. "There will be an obstacle course set up for the race. Participants must navigate through the various sections of the course in order to reach the finish line. To qualify, you must be an eighth grade boy. The first runner who crosses the finish line will be declared the winner. Please keep in mind that good sportsmanship is extremely important. Any runner who fails to demonstrate good sportsmanship will be disqualified. This rule will be strictly enforced. The race will be held next week in the boys' gym.

I have one more announcement –

The winner will receive a magnificent trophy."

After school, Butch saw me walking home and came running over to talk to me. Butch said with a mean-spirited tone, "You better not enter the race. If you do, you will suffer the consequences. You're a smart guy, you know what I mean."

I certainly understood what Butch meant when he said I would suffer the consequences. He meant he would beat me up if I decided to race. Butch was again bullying me.

I started thinking and was puzzled. Why did Butch want me out of the race? I knew Butch wasn't entering the race because he was a very slow runner and had no chance of winning. So why does he care if I enter the race? All of a sudden, it hit me. It was like a light bulb went off in my head. Everyone knows that Zack and I are the fastest runners in school. The reason Butch didn't want me to race is that he wanted his friend Zack to win. Butch thought if I were out of the race, Zack would win.

This race was a dream comes true. A chance to prove I was the fastest runner in school. I wanted more than anything to win the race. I didn't care about Butch's threats; I decided to enter the race.

In order to participate, each runner had to register and sign a form certifying we carefully read the rules and instructions. The school created a registration desk where we could go to complete the registration process. Ten boys registered and entered the race.

Finally, the day of the race was here.

Before the race started, Mr. Robinson explained the rules and instructions. "There are four phases in the race," he said. "For Phase One, there are four red cones placed in a zigzag pattern. Each runner must run between the cones, following the pattern. For Phase Two, there are hurdles runners must jump over. For Phase Three, there is a wall runners must climb over. For Phase Four, you will find cones lined up in a straight line. This final phase will be a fifty-yard dash. Runners must sprint as fast as possible to achieve the best possible time."

Mr. Robinson continued, "Initially each runner will take a turn running the course. I will use a stopwatch to record your time. The two runners with the fastest times will face off against each other. The course is large enough to accommodate both runners. The final phase, the fifty-yard dash, will determine the winner."

Mr. Robinson then shouted, "Let the Race Begin!"

One by one each boy ran the race. We ran through the zigzag cones, jumped the hurdles, climbed the wall and sprinted to the finish line. When it was my turn to run, I walked past Butch. He stared at me with the look of a monster and said with a terrifying grin, "You're going to be sorry you entered the race." I ignored his latest threat and ran the race.

After all the runners completed the race, Mr. Robinson announced the runners with the two fastest times.

He said, "Joseph and Zack ran the fastest times and will now compete against each other. This will be the final race to determine the winner."

All the boys lined up next to the cones along the final stage of the race. Zack and I went to the starting line. Zack looked at me with a cold, intense, malicious stare. At that moment, if looks could kill, I would've been ten feet under. Mr. Robinson then told us to get down in our runners stance.

He said with a very **LOUD** voice –

"R-E-A-D-Y, S-E-T, G-O!"

We both took off. We ran through the zigzag cones, cleared the hurdles and jumped over the wall. After completing the first three phases of the race, we arrived at the last phase in a virtual tie. We started to run the fifty-yard dash and I began to pull away. I was thinking to myself, I'm going to win. I could taste victory. I was so focused on winning I didn't notice that someone standing next to the cones stuck their leg out in front of me. All of a sudden, before I could cross the finish line, I tripped and crashed to the floor. I scraped my hands and knees. I was bleeding a little, but, except for my pride, I was okay. I didn't know who tripped me, but everyone including Mr. Robinson saw it was Butch.

Mr. Robinson, who rarely got angry, was furious. His face turned brilliant red, similar to the color of my mom's electric red lipstick and his eyes began to expand rapidly and looked like giant bulging googly eyes. He screamed, "Butch, what you did was cruel, insensitive and dangerous. Joseph could've been seriously hurt."

Mr. Robinson dismissed the class and escorted Butch upstairs to see Sister Superior. Somehow, Sister Superior already knew what had happened. We all thought God told her.

Sister Superior was outraged. She yelled. Actually it was more like a bloodcurdling scream. "Butch, how could you commit such a terrible act? Joseph could have been badly hurt!" Sister, realizing she was screaming uncontrollably, began to calm down a little. She continued, "Butch this is very serious. I'm very disappointed in your behavior. This is not the first time you've acted this way. What is really frightening to me is that you seem to show no remorse. You don't appear to be sorry for what you've done. I hope your parents can make you understand the severity of your actions. I will pray for you, but remember, God only helps those who help themselves." Sister spoke to Butch's parents and he was suspended for three days.

The next day in class, Sister Superior told everyone what had happened and that Butch received an out-of-school suspension.

I'm a little ashamed to admit this, but I was happy Butch was suspended. He got what he deserved. I was thinking maybe now he will finally stop bullying people.

Although I was happy Butch was suspended, I was still sad I lost the race. I wanted to win so badly. I was so close. Just then, Mr. Robinson came into the classroom with the trophy in his hand. He said to Sister Superior, "Sorry to interrupt your class, Sister, but I have a special announcement. I'm here to announce the winner of the race. I'm happy to announce the winner of the eighth grade race is Joseph Minnow."

At that moment my body went numb, I was overcome with joy. Mr. Robinson continued, "Although Zack crossed the finish line first, Joseph was ahead of Zack, heading towards the finish line when he was tripped. If this blatant act of unsportsmanlike conduct did not occur, Joseph would have easily won the race."

Mr. Robinson called my name to come to the front of the class. He then handed me the trophy. All my classmates, except Zack, started to clap. This was one of the best moments of my life.

THE FASTEST BOY IN SCHOOL TROPHY

7

The Lecture

Sister Superior told us she spoke to Father Timothy about our bad and disgraceful behavior and that Father was going to speak to us about how wrong it is to bully someone. Sister told us she prayed that Father could nip this in the bud before it gets completely out of control and hoped that prison life would not be part of our future. We were all thinking, *Oh no, not another lecture from Father.*

Father Timothy was a portly man. He was as wide as Sister Superior was tall. He barely fit through the classroom door.

It was about 2 o'clock. We heard Father walking down the hall to our classroom. We always knew it was Father because he made a deafening noise when he walked. He sounded like a giant robot that weighed a ton, walking slowly, lifting one foot at a time, each foot making a thunderous sound as it touched the floor. It really wasn't that loud, but as kids we exaggerated a bit.

Finally, Father appeared. He wore a brown robe with a long rope tied around his waist. He had very little hair, only a whisper around his ears and a small ring around the back of his head.

Father Timothy

We were all thinking, *Oh no, this is it, time for his lecture.*

We all dreaded his lectures because they were always long, dry, methodical and extremely boring. We used to say; "If you could bottle him, you could sell him as sleeping pills." His lectures were always forty-five minutes long. He would never look at a clock, but somehow, he would always speak for exactly forty-five minutes. Father always seemed a little uncomfortable when speaking during his lecture. He would always start by saying, "**Children, it has come to my attention,**" and would then include the topic of the moment. In this case he said, "Children, it has come to my attention that we have bullies in this school. Bullying is against everything we stand for in our school. More importantly, this is a sin in the eyes of God." We didn't know for sure if this was an actual sin, but we believed everything Father told us, so we all believed bullying is a sin. Father continued. "For those of you who don't know what a bully is, I will explain." Father then went on to say –

"Bullying is when you physically or verbally abuse a person or group of people or damage their property or possessions. So, when you humiliate someone for any reason, threaten or physically hurt someone, that is bullying."

We all understood what he meant. Father continued. "When you bully someone, you also bully yourself." This is where he lost us. We just didn't understand this logic. This would happen every time Father spoke to us. There was always something he said that we didn't understand.

Father continued to lecture us on why we should never bully anyone, until he used up all of the forty-five minutes. When Father finished, we were all exhausted from listening to the lecture.

8

The Eighth Grade Dance

It was Friday and we were all happy and in a good mood because the weekend was almost here. Even Sister Superior seemed a little giddy. Little did we know the day was about to get better. Sister said exuberantly, "I have wonderful news. In four weeks the school will be sponsoring the annual eighth grade dance." I didn't know what sponsoring meant, but all I cared about was there was going to be a dance. Sister continued. "The dance will be held in the school auditorium. Furthermore, you will all have the opportunity to help make the dance a success. There is a lot of work that needs to be done before the dance. You can all help in the planning and preparation. There will be a variety of committees set up which you can sign up for to make this year's dance the best ever. The committee's are:

- ❖ **Decorations**
- ❖ **Music Selection**
- ❖ **Lighting**
- ❖ **Table Arrangement**
- ❖ **Food & Beverage Selection**
- ❖ **Transportation**

I found out from one of Katie's girlfriends that Katie was planning to sign up for the decoration committee. I really liked Katie and I wanted to ask her to the dance. I couldn't wait for class to end so I could sign up for the same committee. I didn't know exactly what my responsibilities would be, but I didn't care as long as Katie was there. I kept staring at the clock wishing for the bell to ring.

Finally, the bell rang. Excitedly, I jumped up and ran to the teacher's room and quickly signed up to join the Decorator's Committee. I thought, *wow, this is fantastic. I now have the opportunity to ask Katie to go to the dance with me.* Lately, I'd been spending most of my time thinking about Katie.

All of a sudden it hit me. I started to feel nervous and my palms were sweating. I felt this way because I was thinking, *oh my God, I actually have to ask Katie in person to go to the dance with me. How will I find the courage to ask her? How can I get over my shyness? What if she says No? What if she says Yes? This would be my very first date.* I started to hyperventilate.

I then said to myself, "Joseph, calm down. You're acting like a lunatic. There is plenty of time to figure out exactly how to ask Katie to go to the dance."

When I got home from school I asked my mother if I could have a calendar for my room. She asked why I wanted one. I said, "I'm going to hang it up and circle the date of the dance."

She said okay and bought me a calendar. I guess she noticed how excited I was about the dance. Moms always notice stuff like that.

Well, it's Monday already and I'm back in school. Before class started, all the kids were discussing the upcoming dance and who joined what committee. In class, I found myself thinking about Katie again and how I was going to ask her to the dance. Sister, because she notices everything, realized I was daydreaming and not paying attention. She looked at me and said in an annoying tone, "Joseph, you are not paying attention."

She asked me what I was thinking about. I said, "I'm thinking about the dance."

Sister said, "I know you are all are excited about the dance, but now is not the time to think about that. Now we all need to pay attention to today's lesson."

I said, "Yes, Sister. Sorry, Sister." I knew she was right, but I could not stop thinking about the dance, and more importantly, Katie.

Next, I did something in my young life that turned into one of my most embarrassing moments.

I wrote a note about asking Katie to the dance and passed it to my best friend Mike, who was sitting next to me. I bet you can figure out what happened next. Sister, with her built in sonar and radar, noticed I passed the note to Mike. The next words Sister spoke sent chills down my spine. Sister said, "Mike, what do you have in your hand?"

Mike trying to downplay the whole thing said, "It's just a piece of paper, Sister."

Sister replied inquisitively, "It looks like a note to me. You know we are not allowed to pass notes in class. What could be so important that it could not wait until after class?" She then said to Mike, "Stand up and read the note out loud, so we can all hear what is so important that couldn't wait until after class."

As instructed, Mike stood up and with his voice quivering and knees shaking, read the note. "I'm going to ask Katie to go to the dance with me. Let's meet after school to discuss."

Sister then said, "Will the person who wrote the note stand up."

For a moment I couldn't move a muscle, nervousness took complete control of my body. I was shaking like I had the chills. I found it extremely difficult to stand up. I felt disoriented and a little woozy. As the feeling in my legs slowly began to return, I gingerly stood up and said, "I wrote the note."

Sister walked over and stood in front of Mike and myself. She looked at me dubiously and said, "Joseph, I'm surprised at your childish behavior. I thought you knew better." She then looked at both us and said, "As punishment, you both must stay after school with me today." Mike said, "But Sister, I didn't do anything wrong."

Sister replied, "Yes you did. You accepted the note during class. You are as guilty as Joseph."

I thought it was totally unfair for Sister to punish Mike for my wrongdoing.

Apparently, Sister disagreed with my thinking.

After school we met Sister in the classroom. She said, "Boys, sit down and reflect on what you did. Stay seated in absolute silence until I tell you it's okay to leave."

So, that day after school, we sat in complete silence until Sister finally said we could leave. As we were leaving, Sister asked us if we learned from this experience. We said, "Yes," however it wasn't the type of lesson learned Sister was hoping for. We thought, *next time when we pass a note don't get caught.*

The next day in school, I was worried about Katie's reaction to the note. I thought, *not only did I embarrass myself, but I embarrassed Katie as well.* How could I possibly ask her to go to the dance with me after what happened?

I again felt like my life was over. Boy, did I mess up.

I decided it would be best to avoid Katie at all costs. When school was over, I was going to run out of the classroom and go directly home. However, when the final bell rang, something remarkable happened that took me by complete surprise. Katie rushed over to me and said, "Joseph, I would love to go to the dance with you." At that moment, I was the happiest boy on earth. Hearing those few words from Katie was like winning the bingo jackpot, hitting the winning home run, scoring the winning touchdown and getting a hole in one, all wrapped up together.

Katie then said, "My parents won't allow me to date, but I can hang out with you at the dance. Is that okay?"

I said, "Okay, that's fantastic. I will meet you at the dance. I thought you would be mad at me because of the note."

Katie said, "Mad? No, silly. I thought the note was very sweet. I was flattered."

The next few weeks were great. I worked on the decoration committee with Katie. Every day after school we decorated the auditorium with balloons, streamers and decorative posters. We had so much fun together.

I used my calendar to keep track of the days until the dance. Each day when I got up in the morning I would cross off another day.

The day of the dance was getting close and I was trying to decide what to wear. I wanted to wear something cool; something special that would set me apart from the other kids. One day while shopping with my mom, I spotted this jacket. It was brown with long fringe hanging from the sleeves. I said, "Mom, this jacket is perfect." I could tell she didn't like the jacket, but somehow I managed to talk her into buying it for me.

My Perfect Jacket

Now I was all set to go to the dance. To me, the stars were all aligned, as they should be. Everything was right in the world.

The last time I checked the calendar I saw the dance was only a few days away. I thought to myself, "Soon, I'm going to have the best day of my life."

Unfortunately, what happened at the dance would turn out to be one of the worst days of my life.

It's Saturday and I just woke up. I knew it was the day of the dance, but I looked at the calendar anyway. It was a thrill just to see the date. Finally, the day I've been waiting for. Today is the day of the dance!

At 4 o'clock I got dressed, spent about one hour combing my hair, put on my new jacket and off I went. When I arrived, the auditorium looked fantastic. The balloons and streamers looked even better the day of the dance. The strobe lights were on and the music sounded great. I looked around the room, but didn't see Katie. I noticed that all the girls where standing on one side of the room and the boys were standing on the other side. I walked over to where the boys were hanging out.

When Butch saw me, he immediately started to bully me. He made fun of my jacket. He said I looked like the television cowboy Roy Rogers and asked me, "Where is your horse?" I just ignored him.

Then it happened. Katie arrived.

All of a sudden, I didn't care what Butch said or did. At that moment, only Katie mattered.

She wore a white dress with pink trim and a shiny pink bow in her hair. Her pink lipstick perfectly matched the color of her pink bow. She looked like an angel, a vision of loveliness. I just stared at her for a while. Her beauty took my breath away. I was awestruck.

I was the first boy to leave the boys' side of the room. I slowly began walking towards Katie. When she saw me, her eyes grew larger and appeared to burst with happiness; then, her delicate lips slowly transformed into a beautiful Mona Lisa like smile. Her subtle smile pierced my heart and soul. Happiness saturated my entire body. I was so focused on Katie, I didn't notice Butch's friend Zack sneak up and kneel down behind me. To my utter surprise, Butch pushed me and I fell backwards over Zack. When I fell, I hit my face on the side of the table.

Suddenly, my nose started to bleed.

Katie saw what happened and ran over to me. She paused a second and yelled at Butch. *"Why do you have to be such a bully?!"* She started to help me up and to my horror, as I got up, blood got all over Katie's dress. Katie started to cry; her beautiful dress was ruined. When I looked up I saw Butch, Zack and the rest of Butch's friends all laughing at me. Katie was so upset she called her mom, who picked her up and took her home. I wasn't feeling well and called my mom to pick me up as well.

What a nightmare. I can't believe what had happened.

What could have been the best day of my life turned into one of the worst days of my life.

Another bad thing happened. From that day on, Butch and some of his friends would continue to bully me.

Over the weekend, all I could think about was, *how could I ever face Katie again?* I was so embarrassed by what had happened. I didn't know what I was going to say to Katie. Although what occurred at the dance wasn't my fault, it didn't matter; it happened to me and Katie was part of it.

I was very, very unhappy.

9

Katie's Party

As usual, Monday morning came too quickly. I was off to school. On my way to school, I was trying to think of what to say to Katie after what happened at the dance. I struggled to find the right words and nothing came to mind that made sense. As a result, this is the second time I thought it would be best to not say anything and to avoid Katie for a few days.

When I arrived at school, to my surprise, Katie came running over to me as soon as she saw me. She said with a sympathetic look, "Joseph, I feel so bad about what happened at the dance and I want you to know none of it was your fault."

I said, "Thanks for being so understanding. I'm sorry your dress got ruined."

She said, "Don't worry about it. My mom was able to clean my dress, so it looks good as new." I was thinking, *boy, did I luck out*. Katie is the best person ever. Katie then said something that made everything good again. She said, "Because of what happened at the dance, my mom said I could have a party this Saturday and invite all my friends and you are the first to be invited."

I gushed. "That's fantastic! I would love to come to your party." I was on Cloud Nine. At that moment, something occurred to me that I thought was very ironic. Butch bullying me actually brought Katie and I closer together.

Who would've thunk it? Boy, I didn't see that coming. That night I could hardly sleep. I was so excited thinking about the party.

It's Saturday and I can't wait to go to Katie's party. This time I decided to dress more conservatively. I went back to the basics. I wore a white shirt and jeans. My mom drove me to Katie's house. When I arrived Katie opened the door. For a few seconds, I just stood there, motionless; my eyes remained fixated on her. Again, she looked beautiful. She introduced me to her parents. A few of my friends were already there, so I went over to talk to them. Katie continued to open the door to greet guests as they arrived.

Then, something terrible happened.

I saw Butch at the front door. **GASP!**

Instantly, I got a sickening feeling in the pit of my stomach. How could this be? Butch wasn't invited. Apparently, that didn't matter to Butch; he came to the party anyway. I guess this is something else that bullies do; they go to parties when not invited. Katie was too nice of a person to turn him away, so she invited him in.

It did not take long before Butch started to bully some of the guests. I was dancing with Katie and not paying attention to Butch. Unbeknownst to me, Butch was making fun of the way I was dancing and he made fun of my friends as well. Katie mentioned she was thirsty, so I offered to get her a drink. Her mom made punch, so I went to the punch bowl to get some. Butch saw me and came over towards me. I had a bad feeling this was going to be trouble. Butch asked me why I was pouring two glasses. I told him one glass was for me and the other was for Katie. Butch got mad that I was getting a drink for Katie (unfortunately for me, he liked Katie, too). Suddenly, he grabbed one of the glasses and threw it at me. The punch went all over my shirt and changed the shirt color from white to pink. Butch didn't realize that Katie's parents just entered the room and witnessed what had happened. Katie's father thought we were both at fault and told us both to leave. Katie begged her father to let me stay, but he would hear none of it. He said forcefully, "Joseph must also leave." I called my mom, who came over and picked me up.

On the way back home all I kept thinking about was, *it happened again. Butch managed to ruin everything. Will he ever stop bullying me? What could I do to make him stop bullying me?* This seemed like an impossible task. I thought it would be easier to boil

91

the Atlantic Ocean with a cigarette lighter than to find a way to make Butch stop bullying me. I said to myself, "I don't deserve to be treated this way. I did nothing wrong but I didn't know what to do." I wanted to ask someone for help, but for some reason I just couldn't bring myself to do it.

Eventually, I would come to regret my decision.

10

The Class Trip

One day, we noticed flyers posted all over the school. We began to read them. The flyers stated there would be an eighth grade class trip to the Rocking Horse Dude Ranch. None of us had ever been to a dude ranch, but we quickly realized two things –

First, there will be horseback riding and second, we will be off from school for a few days.

Our eyes were drawn to the words Rocking Horse Ranch and horseback riding. It was like we were in a hypnotic trance. When we finally regained our composure, we continued to read the text in its entirety. To our delight, we quickly discovered there were a variety of fun activities. Uncontrollably, we started screaming. We were jumping up and down like maniacs; we were delirious. The activities were —

- ❖ **Swimming**
- ❖ **Fishing**
- ❖ **Softball**
- ❖ **Archery**
- ❖ **Boating**
- ❖ **Horseshoes**
- ❖ **Basketball**
- ❖ **Hiking**
- ❖ **Hayride**
- ❖ **Bonfire**

We all started to think of the activities we wanted to do first.

Some wondered if it was possible to do all the activities. For me, the first thing I thought about was the hayride and the bonfire. I imagined these activities would bring Katie and me closer together. I began dreaming of sitting next to her on the hayride and holding her hand at the bonfire. The mental image reminded me of the TV show, "New Adventures of Spin and Marty". The show featured stories about kids having fun on a dude ranch. My first crush was Annette Funicello, an actress on the show. But hey, I knew she was an actress on TV and unapproachable, unlike Katie, who was the real thing and absolutely approachable. Enough reminiscing, let's get back to reality.

It was the day of the class trip. You could feel the excitement in the air. It felt like the opening kickoff to a championship football game. We were consumed with excitement. The school arranged for a bus to take us to the dude ranch. We boarded the bus and off we went. A few class mothers accompanied us as chaperones.

Most people tried to avoid sitting next to Butch and his friends. Unfortunately, the bus was so crowded, that some of us had no choice. If you were unlucky that day, you sat next to Butch and his pals. As expected, Butch and his friends would bully anyone sitting next to them. They were sly like a fox trying to steal eggs from the chicken coop. When a class mother wasn't looking, they would act like two year olds. They would pull your hair, pinch the back of your neck and ears, insult you because of the way you dressed, call you disgusting names, etc. When a class mother saw their bad behavior, they would repeatedly tell them to stop, but they wouldn't listen. I wondered, *don't these guys ever get tired of acting this way?*

Apparently not.

Thankfully, we finally arrived at the ranch.

We were introduced to the ranch hands and they showed us to our rooms. We planned to spend two nights at the ranch.

The first activity of the day was of course, horseback riding. We all lined up to take our turn getting on our horse. Jimmy, a boy with a physical disability, was told he couldn't ride. Apparently, his disability prevented him from riding. Jimmy felt terrible. Sadness and disappointment instantly gripped his face. Typically, despite his disability, Jimmy is able to do most activities as the rest of us. However, riding a horse was too risky. Butch, who happened to be standing in line next to Jimmy, began to bully him. He said, "Jimmy, you're acting like a sissy for not insisting to ride. Why don't you act like a man?" Butch then called him a slimy worm and a jellyfish with no backbone.

Butch did something I thought was even below his level of indecency. He made fun of a person with a disability. Butch somehow managed to sink to a new low. Is there no limit to his insensitivity? Jimmy was feeling bad enough, but Butch found a way to make him feel even worse.

My friends and I told Jimmy he could hang out with us after we get back from horseback riding. Jimmy felt better knowing we wanted him to join us later.

We were all on our horses and our guide directed us to follow him on an adventurous trail through the woods. It was a beautiful sunny day, not a cloud in the sky. Perfect for riding. During our ride, we couldn't help but notice nature all around us. It permeated our senses. The gentle flow of the wind was both delightful and refreshing. I closed my eyes for a moment and it felt like I was floating on air. The rays of the sun reflecting off the moisture that collected on the leaves produced an amazing rainbow-like display amongst the treetops, similar to the glittering iridescent colors that appear when the sun shines against the spray of a waterfall. On some of the trees, the sudden burst of sunlight jabbing through the branches looked like the glimmer and glow you see on those small white flashing holiday lights. Nature's light show was better than any light show from any rock concert.

We saw owls, hawks, eagles, deer and groundhogs while crossing crystal clear streams. Our ranch guide identified the wildlife so we wouldn't miss all of what nature had to offer. It was a wonderful experience to travel on horseback and be in touch with nature. I never appreciated nature before and I was in awe. As we continued to ride, a hypnotic calm took hold of me. I was euphoric. We rode for hours; however, it only felt like minutes. Somehow, time has little meaning in the woods.

Unfortunately, all good things must come to an end. It was time to go back and we returned to the ranch.

We now had free time to do any activity. My friends and I met up with Jimmy, who was very excited to join us.

First, we played basketball. After basketball we went fishing and we all caught fish. Lastly, we played tennis. We had a great time. After tennis we went back to our rooms to clean up for dinner. When we were ready, we headed down to the mess hall. There were platters of turkey, roast beef, mashed potatoes, a variety of vegetables and a large table covered with desserts. The food was fabulous. One of the desserts was appropriately named Angel Food cake; it felt like we were in food heaven.

The large dining room had a rustic country feel. The ceiling contained enormous wooden beams and hanging from the beams were long black whips, dried cactus plants, deer antlers, horseshoes, pictures of famous cowboys (John Wayne, Roy Rogers, Tex Ritter, etc.) and cowboy boots with spurs and a saddle. The entire staff was dressed in Western gear, complete with cowboy hats and red handkerchiefs. It was like being in a John Wayne western movie. The whole dining experience had the feeling of dining out in the open range. It was fantastic.

The only thing missing was I didn't get to spend any time with Katie. I hung out with the guys and she hung out with girls. I kept thinking, *I can't wait to be with Katie.*

The good news is there were two planned events that night; I thought this could be my big chance to be with Katie.

First came the hayride. After dinner, there was an open wagon that was pulled by two of the biggest horses I'd ever seen. On top of the wagon were bales of hay. Luckily, there were plenty of secluded spots. When I got on the wagon I saw Katie and immediately raced to sit next to her. When we were all seated, our guides began to drive the wagon around the entire ranch. As the sun began to set, you could feel the warm air all around you. I took a deep breath and I could almost taste the clean fresh air. The sky looked like the Aurora Borealis with a spectacular assortment of colors that had the uncanny resemblance of light passing through a prism. It was like I was looking at the sky through a kaleidoscope. The only picture more beautiful was that of Katie. Her sheer beauty was intoxicating. She looked at me. My heart fluttered. It seemed to stop for a second and then started to beat again. Her stare consumed me; it touched every fiber of my being. As I continued to gaze into her eyes, it felt like my heart was melting as my body temperature continued to rise. I drew a sharp breath and had to pinch myself to make sure I wasn't dreaming. Suddenly, life just got better.

I wanted to put my arm around her. I thought to myself, *should I ask her if it would be okay to put my arm around her?* Do I not ask her and just move my arm very slowly, inch by inch, or move my arm quickly before she has time to stop me? Suddenly, I overcame my fear and simply put my arm around her.

What happened next was an unexpected, but delightful surprise.

Katie held my hand. This was the first time I held a girl's hand or put my arm around a girl who wasn't a relative or my sister. It's hard to find the words to express how I was feeling, but here goes. The pressure of her gentle touch felt amazing. It was like being touched by an angel. I was overwhelmed with joy and happiness. My heart was pounding so fast and loud I had trouble catching my breath. The sound was deafening. I was tingling all over as happiness spread throughout my body and soul. I felt like an emotional time bomb ready to explode. It was like I was in heaven without dying.

I didn't know it at that moment, but my day would actually get better. Much better. There I was, looking at Katie, gazing into her eyes. Her eyes looked as blue as a gleaming blue sapphire gemstone; they shined like stars sparkling in the night sky. Her beautiful golden hair was more radiant than the brilliance of a 24-carat gold necklace. *All of a sudden, I kissed her*. It was like I didn't have control of my actions. Her beauty possessed me. I'd been thinking about kissing her for so long, I just couldn't resist. It felt like an unknown force pushed me towards her.

I'm not sure how Katie felt, but to me it was the greatest moment of my life. I wouldn't trade that moment away for anything, not fame or fortune or the first issue of a Superman comic. I wanted the hayride to last forever. But alas, we had to return to the ranch.

On the way back to the ranch, we could see the bonfire burning brightly.

We got off the wagon and formed a circle around the bonfire. It was an impressive sight. The warm glow of the fire paled in comparison to the warm feeling I felt in my heart for Katie. The fire was captivating. We were in awe by the power and beauty of the flames; it touched all of our senses. You could be hypnotized by its mesmerizing glow. The staff handed out marshmallows and we began roasting them on the fire. There I was, holding hands with Katie while roasting marshmallows. I was living my dream. My dream became reality. It was the perfect end to a perfect day.

Amazing!

However, there was one unfortunate event that happened. Butch saw me holding hands with Katie. He was furious – overcome with jealousy. Remember, Butch also had a crush on Katie. I didn't know it at the time, but Butch was planning his revenge.

The next morning when I woke up, I was still thinking about the great time I'd had last night with Katie. It was a night I will never forget.

After breakfast, we were scheduled to go horseback riding again. We went to the stable to get the horses. Once on horseback, our guides took us on a new trail. At first, I didn't realize Butch was riding directly behind me. For a while everything was fine. All of a sudden, I felt something hit me. I looked around, then looked behind me and saw Butch laughing. I noticed he had rocks in his hand. I quickly realized that Butch threw a rock at me. Due to an incredible circumstance of bad luck, our guide was a few horses ahead of me and didn't see what happened.

Then, a terrible thing happened.

The next rock Butch threw hit my horse. The horse got startled and suddenly bolted ahead. The horse began to gallop with incredible speed. I was bouncing violently up and down in the saddle. I looked like the silver ball in a pinball machine. Our guide saw my horse run past him. Instantly, he came after me. He managed to catch up to me and stop my horse. In another minute I would have fallen off the large animal. I was amazed by how well the ranch guide could ride. Wild Bill Hickok could not have done better.

I explained to the guide what had happened. When our guide questioned Butch, of course he denied it. No big surprise there. As usual, Butch was not blamed for his bad behavior. Once again, Butch managed to bully me and would completely get away with it. I started to think *sometimes life is unfair.*

We returned to the ranch.

It was now time to leave this magical place out in the country. We boarded our bus and went back home.

I'll never forget the great time I had at the ranch and the special moments I shared with Katie.

11

Graduation Day

The next day we were back in school. I asked myself, "Why is it that all good things end so quickly?" Everyone was very happy because it was the last two weeks of school before the summer vacation.

Sister had another announcement. Enthusiastically she shouted, "Today you will be receiving your yearbook. Please take care of your yearbook. It contains memories that will last a lifetime."

Later that day, the yearbooks arrived. We were all excited.

After school we all looked through the yearbooks. We couldn't wait to see our pictures. When I saw my picture, I thought I looked a little goofy.

Immediately, I turned the page to look at Katie's picture. She looked beautiful. Although the picture was very small, her beauty was enormous and it shined brightly on the page.

We all began to ask each other to sign our yearbook. Naturally, the first person I asked was Katie. I couldn't wait to see what she would write. She didn't disappoint. She wrote, "You are the nicest guy I ever met. I hope we will be close friends forever." After I read this, I was dizzy with happiness and for a moment, it took my breath away.

Katie then asked me to sign her yearbook. I wrote, "I'm so happy we are close friends. You are so sweet. I know will be friends 4 ever. You are my dream come true."

I could've written a book about how I felt, but there wasn't enough space to write on the side of the page.

I began to ask my other classmates to write something in my book. Some wrote something nice, others wrote some silly and kind of corny messages:

Jill wrote, "UR 2Cool 2 Be 4 Gotten."

Jane wrote, "Shoot for the moon. Even if you miss you'll land among the stars."

Alice wrote, "Remember Grant, remember Lee, but most of all remember me."

Glen wrote, "Best friends forever."

Albert wrote, "Never settle."

Donna wrote, "It tickles me, you made me laugh, to think you want my autograph."

Maureen asked me what to write. I told her to write **anything**, so she wrote **"Anything"** and signed her name under it.

Bella wrote:

"I
I am writing this
I am writing this in the corner
I am writing this in the corner of your
I am writing this in the corner of your yearbook."

Then, a terrible thing happened.

Butch Barotti, the class bully, signed my yearbook. He wrote, "You are going to die tonight!" After reading this I had mixed emotions. On the one hand I was thinking, 'I can't die I'm just a kid. However, on the other hand I have to admit I was really scared. What if Butch's prediction comes true? Maybe his comment was some sort of curse or bad omen.'

Later when I got home my mother read Butch's grim prediction. As I looked at my mom, she appeared to be both upset and annoyed. She said, "What Butch wrote is heartless and insensitive. He should be ashamed of himself for writing such an awful comment. My mom paused a moment, looked at me and said in a convincing tone, "Joseph you are not going to die tonight, don't be silly. Everything is going to be all right. Don't pay attention to such nonsense. I replied sheepishly and with disbelief, "Okay mom, if you say so."

It's 9:30, time for bed. It seemed like 9:30 came quicker than usual. There I was lying in bed starring at the ceiling. I couldn't stop thinking about Butch's terrible prediction. My mind was racing with thoughts of fatality. 'What if I have a heart attack, what if I stopped breathing. My mind was consumed with what if scenarios.'

I turned sideways and began to stare at the clock on the night table. As each minute passed I started to believe I was getting that much closer to death. I fought the urge to close my eyes. My eyelids felt heavy, like there were small weights attached to them pulling them down. As time passed I couldn't keep them open. Finally, the inevitable happened, I fell asleep.

The next day morning came like it always does. I slowly opened my eyes and stood still a few minutes wondering if I was still alive. **SUDDENLY**, I leaped out of bed. I began to touch my face, arms and proceeded to touch different items in my room. For a moment I thought, 'Am I really alive, or could I be having an out of body experience.' All of a sudden, I heard my mom call my name. Instantly I ran downstairs faster than I have ever did before. I was never so happy to see my mom. I hugged my mom, something I never do first thing on the morning. My mom said, "Wow what was that for." I replied, "Just happy to be alive mom." I thought to myself, 'I'll never again take life for granted.'

The day went by quickly and I was back in bed. The following day, it finally happened. It's here. **Today is the last day of school!**

It's hard to believe I will be graduating tomorrow. There was a very different feeling about this day. I was both happy and sad at the same time. Happy I would be out of middle school, but sad I wouldn't see some of my classmates.

At last, the big day arrived: _Graduation Day_.

Everyone is assembled in the auditorium. Our parents and other family members are present. Sister Superior and Father Timothy both gave inspirational speeches. Naturally, Father Timothy spoke for exactly forty-five minutes. Then, Father called us one by one to the stage to receive our diplomas. We were all very excited to receive them.

There was a special feeling of accomplishment, something to be proud of. After receiving my diploma, I walked off the stage. I looked at my mom and she was crying. My father said, "Nice job, Son. Your mother and I are very proud of you."

This was the first time I could remember my father saying he was proud of me. His comment was very special. It felt great hearing my father say those words to me.

I thought to myself, what a great day, nothing can ruin this day, not even Butch.

Unfortunately, as it turned out, by the end of graduation, I would feel very sad. It was like I lost something special and would never get it back. I will explain shortly.

The graduation ceremony was over. I told my parents I was going to speak to Katie and I'll be back in a few minutes.

I saw Katie standing in the back of the auditorium. I walked over to her and said, "Congratulations, Katie." We talked about our plans for the summer and began to reminisce about everything that had happened during the year. Katie knew I was planning to attend the public high school in town. I knew Katie was still deciding where to go to school. Her choice was between an all-girl Catholic high school and the public high school. I asked her if she'd made a decision. I could see a feeling of sadness come over her face. It was hard for her to respond. She struggled to get the words out. Finally, she said, "I'm going to the Catholic high school. I don't want to go there, but my parents are forcing me. I really want to go to public school so we can be together."

As I listened to Katie, it felt like someone just kicked me in the stomach and knocked the wind out of me. Suddenly, happiness left my body. This was terrible news. I was heartbroken.

Katie continued with a concerned voice, "I know what's going to happen. You will make new friends and we will drift apart."

Without hesitation I replied, "Katie, there is nothing in this world that will keep us apart. We will see each other after school. I promise."

I didn't want her to know how awful I was feeling. I did my best to calm myself and hide my true feelings. I told her how disappointed I was that we would not be attending the same school and how much I will miss not being with her in school.

I may have fooled Katie into thinking I was okay; in reality, I was devastated.

After realizing Katie and I would not be attending the same high school, *my fabulous day was ruined.*

Although my graduation day was ruined, that summer was one of the best summer's in my life. I spent every moment possible with Katie. We had a great time together. It was wonderful.

12

High School: Ninth Grade – The Fight

Today is my first day of high school. I'm now officially a freshman.

Wow, me, a freshman. I was feeling a bit nervous because I didn't know what to expect. I was worried about everything and started to ask myself questions:

Will I fit in?
Will I make friends?

Will I like my teachers? Will they like me?
Will I get good grades?
Will I overcome my doubts and fears?
Will I get bullied again?

There were so many questions swirling around in my head. The more I thought about them, the more nervous I became.

Little did I know at the time, but I was about to experience many firsts in high school.

It was Monday morning. The day began okay. I got ready for school and walked to the corner of my street to catch the school bus. This was the first first for me. In middle school I walked to school, but now I'd be taking a bus. When the bus arrived, I got on. There was only one person I knew on the bus and that was my cousin Connie. She was a lot of fun. We got along great. I felt better knowing Connie was on the bus with me.

Well, it'd been about a month and so far so good. I'd adjusted to riding on the bus. One funny thing about the bus ride was the bus driver, who happened to be a woman. She was about six feet tall and appeared to weigh about 300 pounds. In other words, she was **<u>GIGANTIC</u>**. She always wore tight, tight clothes that seemed to be two sizes too small. We never knew her name, so we just made one up. We called her **"Bulbous Bialy".** We called her that because she reminded us of an enormous bialy that was about to explode at any moment. (For those who don't know, a bialy is similar to a bagel). In order for her to walk on the bus, the doors had to be opened to their fullest extent. The bus driver's seat was supported by metal springs, and when she sat on it the seat would instantly collapse downward at least eight inches. There was one other curious thing about her: she never said a word, never spoke to us, never said good morning, good afternoon, have a nice day, nothing, not even hello. However, she did one important task very well; she drove us to school safely every day.

While on the bus, I quickly made a new friend (Ron), a boy who lived up the street from me. My classes were okay and I liked most of my teachers. There was one teacher who was very strict and overly demanding, so I wasn't happy about him. However, it could have been worse. Why does there always have to be a least one teacher you are not happy about? I guess that's life.

I felt that I was slowly adjusting to life in high school. I hung out with my new friend and my cousin Connie.

One day in school, Connie introduced me to one of her friends, Nancy Beckman. She seemed okay when I first met her, but I would soon discover she had issues. Later that day, I had lunch with Ron. I told him my cousin introduced me to her friend Nancy. "Oh no. Her last name isn't Beckman, by any chance, is it?" Ron said, as his voice elevated.

"Yes," I replied.

"Nancy Beckman is the most annoying, obnoxious, intolerable, unbearable and unpleasant girl in the entire school," said Ron. "Your cousin Connie is her only friend. She is the only person I know who could put up with her. Your cousin is a saint."

After school, I got on the bus to go home. During the ride home, there was this boy, Xavier Steele, sitting near the back of the bus. Seemingly, for no reason, Xavier began to make fun of Nancy. I thought to myself, not again. This can't be happening. It didn't take long before I would witness someone being bullied. Xavier began to make fun of Nancy and the clothes she was wearing.

Xavier noticed Nancy often wore the same dress. Xavier said sarcastically, "I see you are wearing the same dress again. I call it, **'The give it a rest dress'.** Don't you have any other dresses you can wear or any other clothes for that matter? Don't you get tired of wearing the same clothes all the time? I know I get tired of looking at them."

You could see Nancy was becoming more and more uncomfortable. Her face began to grimace. She kept squirming around in her seat. It seemed like she was sitting on a bed of hot coals. She tried to ignore him; she just sat perfectly still.

Thankfully, the bus arrived at school.

Ron said, "Xavier is the biggest bully in school. He thinks he is better than everyone else. He picks on everyone; boys, girls, freshmen, seniors, it doesn't matter. His friends call him Xman. He seems to be the type of person who enjoys being cruel and insensitive and takes great pleasure in embarrassing people. My sister told me he even bullies his younger brother. She said Xavier punches his brother, takes his toys, sometimes breaks his toys, constantly makes fun of him and bullies him non-stop."

Xman

Xman was best friends with Bob Booker (alias BB), the second biggest bully in the school. Suddenly, Ron became dead serious. He stared at me with an intense look on his face and said, "Joseph, for your own good, stay away from both of them. Avoid them at all costs."

I replied, "I certainly don't want to associate myself with people who act like bullies." I thought *I had enough of dealing with bullies in eighth grade; I don't want to experience that again.*

At the end of the school day, I boarded the bus to go home.

I noticed Nancy was not on the bus; she wasn't sitting in her usual seat. I asked my cousin if she knew what happened to her. "She decided to take the late bus home," replied Connie. Although my cousin didn't know why she took the late bus, I believed the reason was she didn't want to see Xman.

The next morning I boarded the bus for school. I sat next to my friend Ron. I noticed Nancy was back sitting in her usual seat. That's another curious thing I noticed. It seemed that everyone riding the bus would sit in the same seat every day. It's similar to the classroom, where typically everyone sits in the same seat as well. My friend Ron told me he believes the reason people sit in the same seat each day is that we are all creatures of habit. I didn't know if this was true or not, but who am I to argue with that kind of logic.

Xman was sitting in his usual seat, which happened to be next to Nancy. I was hoping he would leave her alone today, since he'd just bullied her the day before.

Unfortunately, I was wrong.

It didn't take long before Xman started to bully her. He again started making fun of her clothes. He didn't stop there. He made cruel and nasty comments. He said, "Hey, Nancy, I'll bet you've never been on a date. I'm talking about a date with a human being.

I can't think of anyone I know who would ask you out." He kept insulting her non-stop all the way to school. It was awful. When we arrived at school, she again raced quickly off the bus.

On each bus ride home, Xman continued his verbal abuse. This went on for weeks. All the kids on the bus thought Xman was acting like a jerk and a bully, but no one did or said anything, mostly because they were afraid.

It's 3 o'clock on Friday and we are all back on the bus headed home for the weekend. Xman again started to make fun of Nancy. This time she began to twitch violently, like she was having spasms. It looked like a small earthquake erupted in her body. She was so upset she started to hyperventilate. She resembled a wounded fish, swimming erratically upside down, struggling to breathe. Her reaction was upsetting everyone on the bus, especially me. I was getting to the point where I couldn't take it anymore. I could no longer just sit there and do nothing.

I stood up and yelled forcefully, "Enough is enough, already. Leave her alone."

Xman looked at me, his eyes narrowed to revel a frightening expression. He replied, "Mind your own business, if you know what's good for you. What are you, her protector?"

"She is my cousin's friend," I said. Suddenly, goose bumps started to pop up all over my arms, some even appeared on my chest. There were so many of them, they looked like the bumps you see on a big sheet of bubble wrap. Luckily, before things got out of control, the bus stopped at my street. As I got off the bus, Xman stared at me intensely with a look that would frighten the bravest of men. Xman said, "You'd better watch your back. I'm your worst nightmare." Little did I know that after I made my comment, Xman instantly became my enemy and was out to get me.

Over the weekend, I thought about what happened on the bus and Xman's words of warning. I thought about Nancy as well. Although she was extremely annoying and obnoxious, she didn't deserve to be bullied. No one, no matter what the circumstances, deserves to be bullied.

I thought about what my friend Ron said. "Stay away from Xman." Although I thought I did the right thing by standing up for Nancy, I worried how Xman would act towards me.

Unfortunately for me, I would soon find out and it wasn't good.

It was Monday morning and I was sitting on the bus, when something unusual happened. Unexpectedly, an older man walked onto the bus. I didn't know it at the time, but the man was Nancy's father. We all looked at each other and wondered why he was on the bus.

Nancy's father walked up to Nancy and asked, "Where is Xman sitting?" She pointed her finger to identify him. Nancy's father slowly walked towards Xman. We all watched with bated breath. For the first time ever, you could hear a pin drop on the bus. The closer he got to him, the more frightened Xman became. This is the first time anyone had seen Xman look scared. He was as nervous as a mouse that inadvertently wandered into a snake pit at the local zoo.

117

Nancy's father closed in on the Xman. He came within an inch of his face. As a matter of fact, it would have been difficult to slip a credit card between their noses. In a slow, deep, raspy voice he said, "The next time my daughter tells me you bullied her or if you even look at her the wrong way, I'll come back and knock your teeth down your throat. This is no threat, it's a promise." Then, Nancy's father turned around and calmly walked off the bus.

After he left, you could cut the tension on the bus with a knife. We were stunned and our stomachs felt queasy. We all felt like we were floating in outer space. It was like we were experiencing zero gravity. Xman was in a semi-conscious state. He had a blank stare on his face. His face looked like a lifeless mannequin on display in a department store window.

We heard that the police were contacted as a result of what happened between Nancy's father and Xman. We never found out if Nancy's father got in any trouble with the law or if Xman got into any trouble. However, after that day, Xman never bullied Nancy again. I thought maybe Xman would ignore me as well. Maybe there's a glimmer of hope.

The next day, I was back at school. It was lunchtime. I was in the cafeteria having lunch with Ron. I saw Xman and his friend BB getting on the lunch line waiting their turn. I was talking to Ron and didn't notice that Xman and BB sat down next to me. "What are you having for lunch today?" asked Xman.

"Chicken soup," I said, knowing that Xman couldn't care less what I was having for lunch.

"It doesn't look like chicken soup. There seems to be something strange in it." He then did something totally disgusting; he leaned over and spit in my soup. BB started laughing.

BB

Xman said, "See, I told you there was something strange in your soup. Remember, Joseph, I told you on the bus to mind your own business. Your interference got me in trouble with Nancy's father."

I was thinking, *what kind of twisted logic is this? What did my interference have to do with Xman getting himself in trouble with Nancy's father? It made absolutely no sense, but I guess this is how the mind of a bully works, always looking to blame someone else as an excuse for their bad behavior.* Xman continued. "You're going to pay the price for meddling in my affairs. This is just the beginning. I will decide when and where I will strike next. You will never know what hit you. I will get my revenge."

The next day during lunch, Xman sat next to me again. This time he dumped the entire container of pepper into my food, rendering it inedible.

After he ruined my lunch for a second time, I told one of the teachers in the lunchroom. The teacher told Xman he could no longer sit next to me. Additionally, the teacher told Xman he is going to keep an eye on him and if he notices Xman misbehaving, he will get a detention.

Finally, Xman stopped bothering me. Well, at least in the cafeteria.

Things quieted down for a while. Xman stopped bullying me and I hoped that going forward he would leave me alone.

I started to make more and more friends in school. My mom and dad both traveled for business. It turned out that for one Saturday a month, both my parents would be away from home. Since they were away from home, I decided to take the opportunity and have friends come over my house to hang out. At first, everything was fine. We would play cards, or board games; we had a lot of fun.

Then, things started to spiral out of control.

My friends and I started to do silly stupid things, mostly acting without thinking. I ignored what my parents always told me, which was to carefully think before doing anything I may regret later.

Predictably, I did not heed my parents' advice.

Each month my friends and I would do something destructive and foolish. For example, my father collected decorative swords. The swords were hanging on the wall in the family room. They were beautiful, gleaming, handsome looking swords. They looked liked they were from the time of King Arthur and the Knights of the Round Table.

I was in another room of the house and failed to notice that two of my friends removed the swords from the wall. All of a sudden, I heard this loud banging and clanging sound. I ran into the family room and looked in horror as my friends were having a sword fight with my father's prize swords. I yelled frantically, "Stop! Stop, guys! Have you lost your minds? You're playing with my father's prize swords. They're not toys you can play with. They are very expensive collectables."

Recognizing I was in a frantic state of panic, they stopped their swordplay. However, the worst was yet to come. When I inspected the swords, they were all badly dented and deformed. They went from looking like brand new pieces of fine cutlery, to old beat up pieces of junk. The first thing that came into my mind was my father was going to kill me.

Later that day, my friends went home. I had trouble sleeping that night because I knew my father would go ballistic when he saw the condition of the swords. I was lying in bed, staring at the ceiling, trying to think what I could possibly say to him. After thinking long and hard, I reached my decision. I would say nothing, hoping he wouldn't notice the damage. I knew this was wishful thinking, but I just couldn't think of anything that would help the situation. I thought that since the swords have been hanging on the wall for years and that he barely looks at them, maybe he wouldn't notice the damage.

A few days went by and everything was working out according to plan. I was just starting to forget about it when one day my dad noticed something looked a bit off when he glanced at the swords. When he inspected them up close, (I was right) he went ballistic. I looked at him in sheer horror. My father started huffing and puffing. He began to inhale and exhale ferociously, making a sound like the noise a submarine makes when surfacing, as air is forced out of its ballast tanks.

My father's face was as ripe as the tomato my mother used last night to make spaghetti and meatballs. He was so mad I thought he was going to kill me. He grabbed one of the swords and started running after me. My mother saw what was happening and began screaming hysterically. Finally, my father came to his senses and stopped chasing me. He then began yelling uncontrollably. "How can you be so irresponsible? How could you be so stupid?" He started to call me worse names and began to swear in Italian. I tried to explain that my friends began playing with the swords before I had a chance to stop them and that it wasn't my fault. My father would hear none of it.

I was grounded for a month.

About a month went by and it appeared that my father forgot about the sword incident. Both my parents were again away on business and my friends were over my house. It was late December and there was snow on the ground. My friends and I thought it would be fun to have a snowball fight outside. The snow was slightly melted, so it was just the right consistency to make a perfect snowball. We all began throwing snowballs at each other.

My friend Rich said, "I have a great idea." I had come to realize from past experience when Rich would say he had a great idea, it usually meant trouble. He went into my garage and found an old bucket. He filled the bucket with snow and proceeded to go into my house.

Next, he did something really foolish. It was something so foolish, it was even below his pedestrian way of thinking.

Rich opened up the sliding glass doors in the family room. The doors were extra wide French sliding doors. He stood in the middle of the family room, reached into the bucket and began to throw snowballs at the guys who were outside in the backyard. This is something you can't make up. My friends are having a snowball fight from inside my house with people outside my house.

I began to yell at them to stop. Initially, my screaming fell on deaf ears. After a while, Rich said to me, "Joseph, you're no fun." He finally stopped.

As a result of the snowball fight, the carpet was soaking wet. The first thing I thought about was my parents are going to be really upset. After overcoming the initial shock of seeing the wet carpet, I tried to think of how I could clean it. There was still some snow on the carpet, so I got a broom and began to sweep it into a dustpan and dumped it outside. It took a while to remove all the visible snow; however, some of the snow melted into the carpet.

Next, I used a towel to soak up as much water as the towel would hold and went over to the sink to wring it out. I did the best I could to dry the carpet. However, it remained very wet. I was worried my parents would notice what had happened when they returned home from their business trip.

Miraculously, I thought of a great idea.

I remembered my dad had a leaf blower in the garage. I got the blower and used it to dry the carpet. To help in the drying process, I turned the thermostat way up, hoping the heat, in conjunction with the blower, would dry the carpet. I used the blower for hours. Finally, the carpet felt totally dry.

Boy, was I lucky; I dodged another bullet.

The next month we were at it again and my friends were over my house. We were sitting around the kitchen table playing cards. Again, my friend Rich comes up with another great idea. He says he is starving to death and we should cook some food. I said there are cold cuts in the refrigerator; we could make sandwiches. "No way," replied Rich. "I want to eat real food. I want to cook something."

He looked in the freezer and pulled out a steak. "This is perfect, exactly what I want to eat."

I said, "Rich, you can't eat a steak. You don't even know how to cook it."

Rich asked my other friends if they wanted steak and they all responded with a resounding, "Yeah, let's cook the steak." I didn't know how to use the oven, but unfortunately Rich did. So, he put the steak in the oven, set the dial to broil and cooked the steak.

When the steak was done, Rich took a dishtowel and grabbed the hot pan from the oven. He started to bring the steak to the table when all of a sudden he dropped the pan on the linoleum kitchen floor. Apparently, the pan was so hot the dishtowel did not provide enough protection from the heat of the pan. I quickly sprang into action. I picked up the steak and hot pan and cleaned the floor. The juice from the steak went all over the floor, so it took me a while to clean it up.

After cleaning the floor, we all ate a piece of steak and everyone was happy. I thought, *whew, I lucked out. Nothing bad happened, even though the pan dropped on the floor.*

I didn't realize it at the time, but something bad did happen. However, I didn't find out until much later.

That night my mom cooked dinner and used the oven. After dinner, she was washing the dishes when she noticed something was sticking to the bottom of the pan. She didn't know what it was and scraped it off. After removing all of it, she noticed there was a small patch of linoleum missing from the floor. It looked like there was a small hole in the middle of the kitchen floor. It didn't take my mom long to put two and two together. She acted like Sherlock Holmes analyzing the evidence. On that day, Mr. Holmes had nothing on my mom. She came to the conclusion that someone cooked something in the oven and when removing the pan, dropped it, resulting in the pan melting a piece of the floor.

Instantly, my mom became irate, yelling in a voice that revealed she was extremely upset. "Joseph, come here immediately!" To make matters worse, she noticed I had a look on my face like the cat that ate the canary. When I looked at my mom, her face looked like she was being tortured, similar to the way my face looks when the dentist tightens my braces. As her face stiffened, her wrinkles became more obvious; she looked both angry and sad at the same time. She asked me, "Did you cook something in the oven?"

"Yes," I said nervously. At this point, I had no choice and told my mother what happened.

My mom said in a serious tone, "Joseph, I'm very disappointed in your behavior. You know you shouldn't use the oven when your father and I are not home." She then became silent and *sometimes silence can speak volumes.* Finally she said, "You're grounded for the next two weeks. I want you to think about how careless and irresponsible you were to let something like this happen."

I thought, *I'm grounded again. At this rate, I'm never going to get out and have fun.*

There was one other time I got myself in trouble with my friends at my house. We were all sitting on the floor in the family room.

126

One of my friends started to throw a football around the room. At first, everyone tossed the football gently. However, before long the throws became harder and harder. As luck would have it, one of my friends failed to catch the ball and the ball hit and broke one of my mother's vases standing on the shelf against the kitchen wall.

I worked hard to clean up the mess. I made sure I picked up all the broken pieces, including the small chips and flakes of glass that spread out all over the floor. However, there remained one glaring problem I could not hide. There was a blank space on the shelf that the vase used to occupy. I had this sinking feeling in the pit of my stomach; I knew I was in trouble yet again.

When my mom got home, it didn't take long before she realized the vase was missing. I closed my eyes for a second in disbelief and told myself this wasn't happening, while at the same time trying to anticipate her next question. She asked me what happened. I explained how it broke. Suddenly, her facial expression changed dramatically. She looked very disappointed. As a matter of fact, her face seemed to scream out "total disappointment."

My mom said intently, "Joseph, when are you going to learn to be more responsible? You're not a little kid anymore. You are a freshman in high school; you have to start acting like an adult. You should be ashamed of yourself. You leave me no choice; I'm going to have to force you to be more responsible. I'm in the process of deciding what to do. Soon, you will know my decision."

I was left wondering what my mother meant by saying she was going to force me to be more responsible. Deep down, I knew my mother was right. I also realized something else. For the first time in my life, I felt ashamed. While in bed that night, I continued to feel bad about my behavior. I fell asleep knowing I let my mother down.

Well, it's Monday morning and I'm on the bus heading for school.

Once in school, I began walking down the hallway towards my locker. Suddenly, out of nowhere, Xman slammed me into my locker. He laughed at me and ran away.

Apparently, Xman found a new way to bully me. He called it, "Stealth Attack." When you are not looking or paying attention, Xman or one of his friends would sneak up behind you and hit or abuse you in some way.

My friend Ron was walking to his next class when BB, who was hiding around the corner, quickly ran behind him and knocked the books and the papers out from under his arms. All his books and papers flew out and spread all over the floor. By the time Ron picked them up, he was late for class. It finally happened. Instead of just bullying me, Xman and BB began to bully Ron as well. Apparently, Ron was being bullied just because he was my friend. This action went on for weeks.

There were other instances as well.

Xman and BB continued their stealth attacks with other students. They would sneak up behind students and violently shove them against the wall. They would trip them hoping they would fall. Additionally, they would run and kick the back of their legs and carry out other acts of physical violence.

After a while, the stealth-like attacks stopped. However, this would be short-lived as Xman and BB would discover new ways to bully you.

After some sinister thinking, Xman thought of a different approach to bullying. He decided he would make up stories about Ron and myself; in other words, just tell lies.

The first lie in a series of lies occurred in math class. After class, Xman spoke with the teacher, Ms. Maranda. He said, "Ms. Maranda, I would like to report someone I caught cheating during our math test. It was Joseph. I saw him copying my answers."

Ms. Maranda said, "Xavier, you are making a serious accusation. Are you certain you saw Joseph cheating?"

"Yes, Ms. Maranda. I know for sure because Joseph was sitting next to me and I could plainly see he was copying my answers."

The next day, Ms. Maranda said she wanted to see me after class. I went back to my seat wondering what Ms. Maranda could possibly want to talk to me about. When class was over, I went over to speak with her. She narrowed her eyes and with a disappointing stare said, "Joseph, I'm surprised and disappointed in your behavior. Xavier told me you were cheating off his test when taking the math test." I gasped, suddenly realizing Xman was at it again.

Nervously, as my voice began to quiver uncontrollably, I tried my best to explain to Ms. Maranda that I didn't cheat. I was so nervous I had trouble getting the words out. I told her Xavier was just trying to make trouble. Ms. Maranda seemed to believe me, but said she was going to keep a watchful eye on me. Ms. Maranda then said sternly, "Know this. Cheating will not be tolerated in my classroom, not on my watch."

This latest incident made me very angry. I thought, *Xman bullied me again. Will this ever stop?*

I told my friend Ron what happened in math class. Ron said with a concerned voice, "I can't believe Xman would do something so terrible as to lie. You should go tell the principal."

I said, "The principal may not believe me. It would be my word against his. I will wait and if it happens again I will speak to the principal."

"Okay," said Ron. "If it were me, I would say something now, I wouldn't wait. You can't keep letting Xman get away with this. If you never speak up he will never stop bullying you."

I said, "Ron, you are probably right."

A few weeks went by and there were no other incidents concerning math class or with Xman. I thought everything was fine.

However, after class, Ms. Maranda told me the principal wanted to see me.

After school I went to meet with the principal, Mr. Handley. When I walked into the office, the secretary told me to sit in the waiting area until the principal was ready to see me. I was so nervous I thought I was going to cry. My stomach felt like I was on a plane that just encountered a massive air pocket. The longer I waited, the more nervous I became. I must have gone to the bathroom five times in ten minutes. A million scenarios were racing through my mind as I attempted to think of a reason the principal would want to see me. I was thinking. "Obviously, I did something wrong, but what could it be?"

Although I was waiting for about fifteen minutes, it seemed like an eternity. Finally, the secretary said, "Joseph, Mr. Handley will see you now." I walked into his office; it looked and felt creepy. It was the type of feeling that made me think the sooner I can take a shower, the better I would feel.

Mr. Handley was standing next to the window. Mr. Handley was a rugged looking, burly man. He stood about six feet five inches tall. He looked like he was chiseled out of solid granite. He had a very deep voice. When he spoke, it sounded as if he was talking from inside a cave. His voice seemed to have a slight echo effect. When I stepped in, he slowly began to walk to his desk and sat down in an enormous opulent leather chair behind a very large desk. He looked at me with a monstrous stare; his eyes looked zombie-like, lifeless, like a person that just walked out of a grave. It seemed as though his eyes were piercing right through me. I tried to hide my fear as best I could.

After a minute, he said, "Mr. Minnow, do you know the vending machine in the cafeteria is damaged?"

I said, "No, Mr. Handley, I didn't know."

"Interesting you say you don't know," said Mr. Handley. "The janitor said Xavier told him he saw you damaging the front of the machine while you attempted to remove one of the food items. Vandalism is a serious offense. I could report this incident to the police." Instantly I replied, "But Mr. Handley, I swear I never touched the vending machine."

Looking puzzled, Mr. Handley said, "Why would Xavier say you damaged the machine?"

I said, "I don't know. He just likes to start trouble."

"Well, since a teacher or a member of the school staff didn't see you damage the machine, I will let you off with a warning this time. I will be keeping my eye on you and will instruct the other teachers to watch you as well," said Mr. Handley.

I thought, *that's great, not only is Miss Maranda keeping an eye on me, other teachers are watching me as well.* As I got up to walk out, Mr. Handley said, "One more thing, Mr. Minnow. Don't let me see you back in my office. I won't be so lenient next time."

I walked out of Mr. Handley's office shaking, angry and upset. I thought, *Xman lied about me again. He continues to find ways to get me in trouble. What should I do to put a stop to this?*

Again, I decided not to do or say anything. How could I let this go on for so long? In my mind I knew I should speak up and tell someone that Xman has been and continues to bully me. Then, a frightening thought entered my mind; I started to believe that maybe I'm a **coward**. Suddenly, I felt ashamed. What an awful feeling to come to this realization. I became deeply depressed.

A week went by and I forgot about the vending machine episode. Then a good thing happened. I met a new friend; his name was Ben. He was the only freshman to play on the varsity football team. Ben was very big for his age. He was also the most popular boy in the freshman class. You know, football hero and all the fame and glory associated with being a football hero.

One day, Ben said to me, "Joseph, I'm having a party this weekend. If you are free, come to the party."

"You're having a party, that's great," I said. "Thanks for the invite." I thought, *wow, Ben invited me to his party. This will give me an opportunity to make new friends.*

Later, I told my friend Ron that Ben invited me to his party. "Boy, are you lucky. I wasn't invited," replied, Ron.

I said, "I'm sorry you weren't invited. I would have more fun if you were there with me."

"Maybe next time," said Ron.

I didn't know if Xman was invited to the party, but I hoped he wasn't. I know Xman was friends with some of the people who hang out with Ben, so I was concerned he might be invited.

It was Friday, the day before the party. I passed Ben in the hallway and said I was looking forward to his party. To my surprise he said, "I heard you were making fun of me and talking behind my back."

I said, "I would never say anything bad about you."

Ben replied, "Whatever. I think it would be best if you didn't come to my party." Then he just walked away. My body felt stiff and numb. I couldn't believe what had just happened. I was overcome with disappointment. Why did Ben un-invite me to his party? I just shook my head in disbelief.

At lunch, I met up with Ron in the cafeteria. Ron told me he overheard one of Ben's friends say that Xman told Ben you made derogatory comments about him. The story (a false one, of course) going around was you said Ben was a lousy football player with no talent. The only reason he was on the team was that Ben's father was a best friend of the head coach and the coach put Ben on the team as a favor to Ben's father. Ben did not deserve to be on the team.

After hearing this, I decided I would discuss the matter with Ben. After school I met up with Ben and told him, "I didn't say anything bad or negative about you; Xman is lying." Regrettably, Ben did not believe me.

Once again, Xman's lies caused me much pain and anguish. I've come to realize it can be extremely difficult to defend yourself against a lie. It's your word against the person spreading the lie. I didn't know what else to do. I felt lost and helpless.

After the party was over, I heard everyone had a great time. Although I was upset I didn't go to the party, I was more upset that Ben didn't believe me and thought I was spreading rumors about him, which is something I would never do.

Well, it'd been quiet for a while and again Xman seemed to stop bullying me. However, he now turned his attention to Ron. He started to spread rumors that Ron had a crush on this girl in school. Her name was Emily and she was the most popular girl in school. She was very sweet and friendly with everyone.

Xman told Emily's friend (Lilly) that Ron said he took Emily on her first date. Lilly listened in disbelief and said, "I don't think so, Xavier. Emily's my best friend and if she went out with Ron she would have told me."

Xman said, "What makes you so sure? You know, there are some things girls keep private."

Lilly was getting frustrated listening to Xman, so she just walked away. Rumors travel fast and soon every girl in the ninth grade was talking about Ron's date with Emily. When Emily heard the news, she became extremely upset.

When school ended, Emily was walking to the bus and saw Ron along the way. "Ron, how could you say such a thing?" shouted Emily angrily. "Your little story has everyone talking about us. How could you make up a lie like that? I thought you were my friend. Is this a guy thing, lying to impress your guy friends?"

Her eyes began to swell with tears. She tried to hold them back but couldn't and she began to cry.

Before Ron could say a word, she ran to catch the bus. Ron felt terrible. He knew Emily's feelings were hurt. Although Ron realized what had happened was not his fault, that didn't seem to matter. The damage was done. It is a helpless feeling knowing at that moment there was nothing he could do to comfort her.

The good news is that eventually Emily discovered it was Xman who was the person responsible for spreading lies. However, it was not before his brazen dishonesty caused much pain and suffering for Emily and Ron. The emotional damage was done.

A few days later, I was on the football field during gym. Mr. Monty taught gym. This was the week we played touch football. The game was two-hand touch. The rules are that the defensive player must touch the offensive player with two hands in order to stop the offensive play. My position was wide receiver. Although I was small for my age, I was a fast runner. During the first play of the game I ran a fly pattern deep down the sidelines. The quarterback threw a perfect pass right into my hands. I caught the ball running full speed and glided into the end zone for a touchdown. It was such a thrill to score a touchdown. The feeling was wonderful. My teammates were jumping up and down, giving me high fives. However, my happiness proved to be short-lived. It so happened that Xman was the defensive player whose assignment was to cover me on the play. You see, after I scored the touchdown, some of Xman's teammates began to make fun of him for allowing me to score. They said sarcastically, "Isn't that the guy you told us was afraid of you? Well, he didn't look afraid when he flew past you for a touchdown. It was more like, take that, in your face, Xman."

Upon hearing this, Xman began to get angry. His teammates managed to push all the right buttons. Unfortunately, Xman decided to take his anger out on me.

On the next play, I ran a crossing pattern over the middle of the field. I caught the ball in front of Xman. Instead of gently touching me, he shoved me extremely hard. It felt like I was hit with the force of a powerful tornado. I felt like Dorothy in the Wizard of Oz when a tornado violently shook and lifted up her uncle's farmhouse. He pushed me so hard that I went crashing to the ground.

Xman stood over me with a triumphant grin on his face and said, "That's the last time you will ever score a touchdown on my watch, you loser."

I got up, shaken, but okay. Since I gained substantial yardage, the quarterback called the exact same play. I ran the same crossing pattern to the middle of the field and caught the ball. Again, Xman hit me extremely hard and I tumbled to the ground. This time, Mr. Monty saw what happened and yelled, "Xavier, you're playing much too rough. You are going to hurt someone, so knock it off."

When the game was over, Mr. Monty spoke to me about the play and told me he wanted to see me after class. Xman saw me speaking with Mr. Monty and as he walked off the field, he stared at me intensely with a vicious and angry look.

After class I went to see Mr. Monty in his office. He said, "Joseph, is there a problem between you and Xavier?"

I said, "I don't have a problem with him, but he seems to have a problem with me. For some reason, he constantly bullies me."

"Do you want me to speak with him about this?" said Mr. Monty. "No, sir," I said. "I will handle this myself."

"Okay," said Mr. Monty. "Let me know if you need my help." Mr. Monty continued, "You know, Joseph, I had a problem with a bully when I was in school and it had a major impact on my life. Do you want to hear my story?"

"Absolutely," I said.

"Okay, let me give you some background information. As you can see by the many trophies on my wall (the wall was adorned with them), I was the star pitcher on both my high school and college baseball teams. I was so good that occasionally my pitches would hit 100 mph on the radar gun. I was so talented that during my senior year in college, the Cleveland Indians offered me a baseball contract to play for their minor league team. The contract was for a large sum of money. The details of the contract stated that I would collect payment at the end of spring training, provided I pitched well. I can't put into words how happy I was about playing professional baseball. It was my lifelong dream.

My friends wanted to take me out to celebrate. About two months before I had to report to training camp, they took me to a local bar and grill. We found a large table in the back of the room. We were all sitting around the table when this guy (Brandon Gilles), who I knew from high school, sat at the table next to me. I hadn't seen Brandon in a very long time. I did remember he was one of the biggest bullies in school. He was known for routinely acting violent. In fact, he was expelled from school because of a violent act. Everyone knew it was best to stay out of his way.

I thought that was a long time ago, surely his behavior must have changed for the better. After all, he was older and hopefully more mature.

I was about to say hello when Brandon looked at me and said, 'So, you think you're a big shot now, since you signed a baseball contract? (Evidently, he'd heard the news). Well, I think you are the same punk I knew in high school.' I couldn't believe Brandon would say something so insulting and insensitive, especially after all these years. I guess for some people, once a bully, always a bully.

I said emphatically, as my voice became more serious, 'I don't feel that way at all. I feel lucky and blessed to have such a great opportunity.' My response seemed to make Brandon angrier. He stood up, walked over to me and said, 'You thought you were a big shot even in high school when you pitched for the high school team.' Thinking back, I seem to recall that Brandon tried out for the team, but was rejected. Apparently, he never got over his disappointment and was taking it out on me.

I said, 'Brandon, I don't want any trouble. Why don't you join us?'

'I don't want to sit with you and your loser friends,' he said.

Unexpectedly, he quickly lunged at me and pushed me down. He completely caught me off guard. We began to wrestle with each other. We managed to gradually get up from the floor. Once standing, Brandon body slammed me hard against the wall. My shoulder and arm hit the wall causing excruciating pain. The pain was so unbearable I lost consciousness.

The next thing I remember was waking up in a hospital bed. The doctor taking care of me said that my shoulder was severely dislocated and my arm was broken. Instantly, I was panic-stricken. I was worried about my pitching arm. My mind was burdened with questions and doubt.

About two weeks had passed and I still couldn't move my arm, let alone throw a baseball. I called my agent to review the terms of my contract. He said the contract is not valid unless I can prove I can pitch well during spring training. 'The good news is you don't have to be ready on the first day of spring training,' he told me. 'You will have time to heal and get back into pitching shape.' He encouraged me to focus on getting better and not worry about the contract.

Eventually my arm and shoulder healed. Finally, I was able to throw a baseball. I started my throwing routine. I could throw the baseball without any pain. Unfortunately, I realized that I had lost velocity off my fastball. The fastball was my best pitch, my ticket to the big leagues; now it was just mediocre. Sensing my career was in jeopardy, I suddenly felt sick to my stomach. I was overcome with insecurity and uncertainty.

A week later I went to the minor league camp for tryouts. Scouts were there to witness my pitching performance. It didn't take long for the scouts to notice I'd lost velocity on my fastball. I could tell by the disappointment in their faces they weren't impressed with my performance. Later, I met with my agent. My worst fears were realized. I was no longer the pitcher I once was; my contract was rendered null and void.

I was devastated. It felt like my life was over. All of my plans, hopes and dreams vanished in an instant. What I'd worked so long and hard for was gone forever."

As Mr. Monty continued to speak, his eyes glistened as he held back tears. His voice began to crack as he became more emotional with every word. He drew a deep breath and said, "I was so distraught, I didn't know what I was going to do.

Then, something good happened.

One of the coaches from my high school team heard what happened and offered me a teaching position at the school. So you see, Joseph, I know firsthand how devastating the actions of a bully can be on a person's life. I often think about the fight. I keep asking myself why did it have to happen. What could I have done differently? Why did we have to pick that particular bar? I didn't deserve what happened to me. Abruptly, all my hopes and dreams came to an end."

After hearing Mr. Monty's sad story, I thought, *bullying can destroy people's lives*. What a sad realization. In my mind I asked myself the same question, "Why did such an awful thing have to happen to Mr. Monty? So senseless."

I told Mr. Monty how sorry I was to hear what happened to him.

"Thanks, Joseph. I appreciate your kind words. Unfortunately, sometimes life can be so unfair."

That night in bed, I had trouble sleeping, thinking about Mr. Monty. One haunting phrase permeated my mind and I couldn't get it out of my head: "***Bullying can destroy people's lives.***"

The next day during gym class, Mr. Monty spoke to Xman concerning his bad behavior. Of course, Xman defended his actions by saying he didn't realize he'd hit me so hard. He said he got caught up in the heat of the moment and adrenalin kicked in. Mr. Monty wasn't buying it and quickly replied, "Don't you dare try to justify your actions. I was there and I saw what you did. You knew you used excessive force when you pushed Joseph. If I ever see you do that again to Joseph or any other student, I will make sure you receive an out of school suspension. I want you to think about that. Remember, Xavier, a suspension will go on your permanent record. Also, think how upset your parents would be if you were suspended. You better shape up."

Xavier didn't say a word and just walked away. He knew Mr. Monty wasn't just fooling around; he meant business. The next day during gym class, Xman was again staring at me with a look that could kill. I didn't know it at the time, but Xman was planning his revenge.

Later, after gym class was over, I was taking a shower. There were only a few guys in the shower room. I didn't realize that when Xman and BB entered the shower area, both were holding towels. All of a sudden, Xman and BB began to whip me with the towels. The towels were tightly wound; they both would flick the end of the towel at me. The force of snapping the towel against me felt like bee stings against my skin. Frantically, I yelled at them to stop, but they just kept hitting me.

Mr. Monty heard the commotion and began to walk towards the shower. Xman and BB heard Mr. Monty coming and they dashed out of there faster than two hypersonic missiles. I walked out of the shower and went to my locker before Mr. Monty could see me. I didn't want him to see the red marks on my body. I quickly got dressed and took the bus home.

When I got home I began to feel very uncomfortable. My mom noticed something was wrong and came into my room. She immediately saw my arms were covered with red blotches. Startled by what she saw she asked, "What happened? Who did this to you? Did you tell a teacher?" I felt like a person on the witness stand under interrogation. My mom acted like the famous TV lawyer Perry Mason.

Reluctantly, I told my mom what had happened. After listening to my story, she called the school and spoke to the principal. Upon hearing the news, Mr. Handley spoke to the other boys who were in the shower the same time I was there. The boys confirmed that Xman and BB hit me with the towels. When Mr. Handley heard this, both Xman and BB received out of school suspensions.

Mr. Handley called Xavier and Bob's parents and told them about their sons' suspensions. The boys' parents were very upset to hear the news. Xavier's mom replied with a heavy sigh. "Mr. Handley, my hope is that one day Xavier will somehow, someway realize how wrong it is to bully people, become a changed man and stop his bad behavior." Mr. Handley replied, "From your lips to God's ears."

As a result of the severity of punishment, I was hoping Xman and BB would finally stop bullying me.

For the next few weeks, things were pretty quiet.

Regrettably, the quiet didn't last very long. While riding home on the bus Xman said angrily, "Joseph, it's your fault I got suspended. If you didn't squeal on me and tell your mother I never would have been suspended. Now, you must fight me. I'm going to take great pleasure in beating you up."

I quickly replied, "It's your fault you got suspended. I was just the victim."

"I don't see it that way," said Xman. "You squealed on me and I don't like squealers. You're a crybaby and a coward. You have no choice but to fight me. If you don't fight me, I will come after your cousin. Are you such a coward you would let me abuse your cousin, instead of acting like a man and fighting me? Are you going to let her suffer on your behalf? You are a spineless jellyfish."

I hesitated for a moment, and then said, "Okay, have it your way. After school on Monday, we fight."

Later, when I saw my cousin, she heard about my conversation with Xman and said with a concerned look, "Joseph, are you crazy? I won't let you get beat up on my account. I will go to Mr. Handley and tell him about Xman. He will stop Xman from bullying you and me."

I said, "You're probably right, but this is something I must do for myself. I'm tired of being bullied, I'm tired of being called a coward and I'm tired of doing nothing. I made up my mind. Win or lose, I'm going to fight Xman."

The next day in school, by the end of first period, everyone knew about the fight. Wow, news travels fast in high school. The

144

entire freshman class was buzzing with excitement. It was pretty unanimous; everyone said I had no chance of winning. I was going to get my brains beat out and my face smashed. The police will have to look at my dental records to identify me.

My friend Ron tried a last ditch effort to talk me out of it. He said, "Joseph, I know you want to prove to everyone you're brave and not afraid of Xman, but please, I beg you, change your mind, don't fight him.

Xman knows how to fight. He's been in fights before. You, on the other hand, have never been in a fight. You don't stand a chance against an experienced fighter. You probably couldn't even beat up my little sister."

I replied, "You're probably right, Ron, but this is something I must do. I want you to understand something. I'm tired of being picked on and of being afraid. I believe the only way to overcome my fears is to meet them head on. Now, I have the opportunity to do just that. The only way to conquer my shy and timid personality is to stand up to and fight Xman. Besides, it's all set. I already agreed to fight him; how would it look if I backed out now? Xman would be right, I would be a coward and everyone in school would think so as well."

As I walked through the hallways on the way to my classes, many people were making ominous comments and were making fun of me. I heard…

❖ **Nice knowing you Joseph.**

❖ I hope you know a good doctor.

❖ Get ready to get your teeth fixed.

❖ I would start saying my prayers if I were you.

❖ Tell your mom to get the phone number of the nearest undertaker.

❖ I hope you know a plastic surgeon.

❖ Can I have your unused binders?

❖ I hope you had a nice life. It's about to end.

❖ Can I borrow five dollars before you die?

It was Sunday night, the night before the fight. There I was, lying in bed thinking, *what did I get myself into? What was I thinking? Maybe I should have my head examined.* My mind was filled with uncertainty and doubt. Maybe the guys were right. What if I don't survive or I get some teeth knocked out or break some bones. My mind was racing with different scenarios and none of them were good.

Monday morning came way too quickly. I decided to wear dark clothing just in case, to hide the bloodstains. I was on the bus and Xman slowly walked past me. What I found curious was he did not look at me or speak to me. One of my friends said Xman never speaks to the person he plans to fight and beat up on the day of the fight.

When I arrived at school, I immediately noticed something was very different. I realized everyone was trying to avoid me and I was getting the silent treatment. There was a strange and eerie feeling in the air. For every class, I kept staring at the clock. I was thinking this is how a criminal must feel on death row waiting to die in the electric chair while hoping the governor would call at the last minute to save him. In the movies, the governor never calls and the same will be true for me; no one is going to bail me out at the last minute from fighting Xman.

Well, it finally happened, the 3 o'clock bell rang for dismissal. When I heard the bell ring, my mind went blank and my thoughts temporality froze. A strange feeling gripped my body. Suddenly, I couldn't feel my arms and legs. I was numb all over and found it difficult to move. As the feeling gradually returned to my extremities I managed to stand up and walk to the bus; however, my legs felt heavy and wobbly, like I was walking underwater. While walking to the bus I was having trouble focusing, I couldn't think straight. I didn't know if this was the result of simple anxiety or intense fear.

On the bus ride home, I noticed the bus was much more crowded than usual. Apparently, there were more people on the bus to watch the fight. The bus driver knew something was going on because with each scheduled stop, people that normally would get off stayed on the bus. Eventually, the bus stopped at the corner next to Xman's house. His parents worked and would not be home until much later. We agreed to fight on Xman's front lawn. Almost everyone got off the bus. There were people who got off the bus a few blocks sooner than their regular stop. They didn't care they would have a long walk home. It was more important for them to watch the fight.

The bus ride seemed much shorter than usual. There I was, sitting all by myself. I was trembling and the back of my neck began to perspire. I thought I was coming down with a fever. It felt like my body was shot up with Novocain. I was a shell of my former self. For an instant, I thought this was not really happening, but seconds later reality set in. Then it hit me, this is really happening. Somehow, I found just enough strength to walk off the bus. I was the last person to get off the bus. Xman was the first to get off the bus and was waiting for me. One thing I noticed: he didn't lack confidence.

There we were, Xman and myself facing each other like two gunfighters in an old western movie, waiting to draw. The tension between us was unbearable. I was a nervous wreck. My heart was beating so fast I thought my chest was going to explode. It felt like someone was trying to cut open my chest with a buzz saw. I was wracked with fear. Xman stared at me; his eyes filled with total rage.

Uncontrollably, Xman came running towards me. He acted like an angry crazed charging Rhinoceros. All of a sudden, the small amount of confidence I had completely vanished. However, at that very moment something remarkable happened, my demeanor changed as well. For the first time I now had the mindset of a fierce warrior. It was like my body was experiencing a reincarnation. Suddenly, I was consumed with mind-altering, intense anger. My only desire was to inflict pain and suffering. I've never felt this way in my entire life. I didn't think it was possible for me to feel this way.

We both acted like opposing soldiers on the battlefield, wanting to attack and kill. We both came crashing against each other. It was like two cars involved in a head on collision.

We wrestled to the ground, pushing, grabbing and poking at each other. Xman quickly put his arms around my head, put me in a headlock and began choking me. Remarkably, my strength seemed to increase the angrier I became. The adrenaline stored up in my body kicked into high gear. My newfound strength allowed me to break free of Xman's grip. I somehow managed to roll Xman onto his back. Gaining the advantage, I began to choke him.

The crowds of kids watching the fight were amazed at what they saw. They couldn't believe I was gaining the upper hand. For a moment they were standing perfectly still in total shock and disbelief. Suddenly, they started to yell and cheer. They acted like an ancient Roman crowd, cheering while watching gladiators fight to the death in the Coliseum.

Xman managed to push himself upwards and escape from my chokehold. He then began to kick me. I was able to block his kicks with my own kicks. Although I was never in a fight, my instincts took over. It was like I didn't have control of my body. I just reacted in self-defense.

Surprisingly, I found renewed strength and was no longer afraid.

Xman sensed I was gaining confidence. Enraged, he quickly started throwing punches, wildly at first, but then his punches found their mark. He pounded me hard in the stomach and ribs. I was in pain and had the wind knocked out of me. I fell to the ground. Although I was in pain, my resolve grew stronger. I saw Xman standing over me, laughing uncontrollably and believing he really hurt me. He seemed to take great pride in hurting me. It was apparent, his joy increased as my pain increased.

Seeing Xman laughing at me served to fuel my determination and stamina. Suddenly, I jumped up. My sudden movement caught Xman off guard. I threw a punch, which happened to clip Xman's nose. To my surprise, his nose started to bleed. Seeing blood, especially his own blood, made Xman go berserk. He started swinging violently, but was completely out of control. Seeing Xman's reaction, I also started to swing uncontrollably. Simultaneously we both lost our minds. We were both in such a frenzy we failed to land meaningful blows. Finally, we grabbed each other and again started to wrestle on the ground.

Then, something unexpected happened. Seemingly out of thin air, someone pulled us apart.

We were both so focused on fighting we didn't notice the police car that pulled up to the street next to us. Apparently the policeman saw us fighting and jumped out of his car to stop us. While separating us, he angrily shouted, "Stop fighting this instant! Break it up. I could arrest you both for disturbing the peace, but I'm going to let you off with a warning this time."

He instructed us to go home and told the crowd to go home as well.

My friends helped me get home safely and then they went home.

I was laying in bed that night thinking about the fight. The first thing I thought about was, *I survived. I actually survived the fight. I was still in one piece. No broken bones, no bloody nose, seemingly okay.*

However, I didn't escape unscathed. I was very sore, had some bumps and bruises and my body hurt all over. Somehow, the pain didn't hurt as much as it should have. I believe my pride in knowing I had the courage to fight Xman played a major role in psychologically healing my wounds and making me feel better.

When my father got home he told me he'd heard about the fight. I had no idea how he found out, but when you get into a fight or do something wrong, somehow your parents always find out. My father said, "Joseph, I understand you were being bullied and that's the reason you got into a fight. But remember this: fighting is never the answer, even if you believe you were justified. The first thing you should have done is to tell someone you were being bullied. If you didn't want to tell your mother or me, you should have told one of your teachers. Next time, and hopefully there will not be a next time, please tell someone. Don't ever let this happen again."

The next day at school I was treated like the conquering hero. All of my friends were giving me high fives and patting me on the back. I was treated like a general returning home after winning a major battle. People I didn't even know were praising me.

I saw Ron and said in disbelief, "Ron, I'm happy to be treated this way, but I didn't win the fight. In fact, I almost lost the fight; at best, it was a draw."

Ron said, "Don't underestimate your accomplishment. Don't forget, you were the overwhelming underdog. Everyone thought you had zero chance and that Xman was going to destroy you and win easily. Some thought you would be disfigured or killed. The odds were greatly stacked against you, but you overcame all the odds. It was a herculean feat."

There was one other amazing and remarkable thing that happened. From that day on, Xman and BB both stopped bullying me.

They would never physically bully my friends or me again.

13

The Book Store

There was a bookstore in school. The bookstore was open for one hour each day after school. I always enjoyed reading, so I would often visit it. In fact, I enjoyed reading so much that I belonged to the book club. We would meet every two weeks to discuss books we'd read. There was a large round table in the store and we all sat around it and talked about the books we found interesting to read. We called ourselves "**The Book Knights**". You know, it's a play on words; "*The Knights of the Round Table*." I know, it's a little goofy.

The first time we met, we went around the table to discuss the first book we'd ever read. When it was my turn to speak I said, "The first book I ever read was, 'The Red Badge of Courage'." The first book read by other club members were…

❖ **20,000 Leagues Under the Sea**
❖ **Treasure Island**
❖ **Tom Sawyer and Huckleberry Finn**
❖ **Great Expectations**
❖ **A Christmas Carol**
❖ **The Hound of the Baskervilles**
❖ **The Green Berets**
❖ **The Man with the Golden Gun**

It was interesting to discuss the books, why we enjoyed reading them, our favorite character, our favorite author, etc.

The other great thing about the book club was we had the opportunity to select some of the books the school would sell in the bookstore. The books selected would first have to be approved by the librarian. We all felt proud when the school approved the book we selected and saw it displayed in the bookstore.

One of my friends, George, worked in the bookstore and told me the person working in the store with him had just quit. He asked me if I would be interested in applying for the job. I said, "No way. I'm having too much fun after school to spend my time working."

I didn't know it at the time, but as I was speaking with George, my mom was speaking with the principal, Mr. Handley. She asked, "I heard there is a job opening in the bookstore. It that true?"

"Yes," replied Mr. Handley.

My mother said, "I'm trying to teach my son to be more responsible. I believe working at the bookstore is a great place for him to learn responsibility."

Mr. Handley said, "Mrs. Minnow, I completely agree with you, 100 percent. Joseph can start working tomorrow."

Later that evening, my mom told me she spoke to the principal. The next words that came out of her mouth were terrifying. She said, "Tomorrow after school you will start working in the bookstore."

I said, "Work? I can't work. I'm not ready to work. I'm too young to have a job."

My mom replied, "Your father and I both worked when we were your age. You brought this on yourself. Do you remember what I told you? I want you to be more responsible. I have been very disappointed with your behavior lately. I spoke to your father and he agrees."

I tried to change her mind, but she wouldn't listen. She said with authority, "I will not discuss this any further. You will start working tomorrow and that's that. Oh, one more thing, I better hear you are doing a good job. Mr. Handley told me he is going to keep me posted."

I could see my mother had made up her mind and when she makes a decision, it's always final. No force on earth could change it.

The next day at school I went to the bookstore and reported for work. I saw my friend George and he said, "Joseph, I can't believe you are working at the bookstore. Yesterday, you told me there was no way you would work here."

I said, "Yah, I know what I said. However, my mom had a different idea. She is forcing me to work here."

George said, "It's not so bad, don't worry. I will show you the ropes, everything you need to know. It will be a piece of cake."

The first day on the job came to an end and somehow I survived. The last task of the day was to take the money collected from today's purchases out of the money drawer and put it into an envelope and take it to the office.

After dropping off the envelope in the office, I took the late bus home.

The first week went by and all went well. I can't believe I'm saying this but I was actually beginning to like working at the bookstore. However, my good feelings were about to be shattered. One day, Xman and BB walked into the store just minutes before closing. I was finishing up for the day and placed the envelope with money on the counter. Xman asked me to help him find a book. After searching the store, I told him we didn't carry the book he wanted to purchase. While I was searching for Xman's book, I failed to notice that BB took the envelope with the money.

After Xman and BB left the store I went over to the counter to get the envelope, but noticed it was missing. I thought I might have misplaced it, so I began to look around hoping to find it. During my search it finally hit me. BB must have taken the envelope while I was helping Xman look for his book.

I ran to the office and explained to the secretary what had happened and that the money was stolen. The secretary asked me if I saw the person who took it. I replied, "No." She said she would discuss this with Mr. Handley.

The next day at school, Olivia Mann (a student) told me she saw BB take the envelope. Olivia was sitting in the back of the bookstore reading and no one noticed her. I asked Olivia to come with me to tell Mr. Handley what happened. Olivia told Mr. Handley she saw Bob Booker (alias BB) take the envelope. Upon hearing the news, Mr. Handley contacted Bob Booker's parents. Mr. and Mrs. Booker arrived at school to meet with Mr. Handley in his office. Mr. Handley said, "I'm meeting with all of you today to discuss money that was stolen from the bookstore. One of the students confirmed that Mr. Booker took the envelope containing the money collected from that day's book sales."

Since Bob was caught red handed, he admitted to taking the money.

Mr. Handley said in an ominous tone, "Bob, I want you to know petty theft is considered a minor offense, but it is still punishable by law. It can be a stain on your record and may cost you further down the road, especially when applying for a job. We take stealing of any kind very seriously. I'm not going to report this to the police this time, but you leave me no choice but to suspend you from school for two days. I hope this bad behavior will not be repeated."

After hearing what Mr. Handley said, Bob's parents completely agreed with the principal's decision. They said they would make sure Bob never does something like that again.

14

Substitute Teaching

Let me take you on another journey. We are now leaving the 60's. That's right, it's time to say goodbye to long hair, hippies, psychedelic music and Woodstock as we morph ahead into the present time. The years have gone by so quickly. It seems like yesterday I was getting on the high school bus. I can't believe that I, Joseph Minnow, recently retired from my job as a Computer Specialist.

As often happens in life, you must make a decision that will have a great impact on your future. In my case, I asked myself, *"What will I do now that I'm retired? What can I do for the rest of my life? Although I'm officially retired I still want to work, to do something meaningful."*

What line of work could I do that would make me happy? The kind of work that would make me say, "I can't wait to get up this morning and go to work." I carefully thought about this. This weighed on my mind for quite some time until one day I woke up and knew exactly what I wanted to do. Out of the blue, it just came to me. I want to be a **SUBSTITUTE TEACHER.**

So, to that end, I became a substitute teacher. Many years have passed since 1965 when I first witnessed bullies; unfortunately, there is one thing that remained the same throughout the years; there are still people who bully other people. Can you believe it, after all these years bullying is still here, thriving, alive and well? You would think after all this time people would be smarter and kinder and that bullying would be gone for good.

Let me tell you about some of my experiences as a substitute teacher and how bullying rose its ugly head yet again.

I was substituting for Mrs. Higgins, who taught eighth grade math. I struggled with math when I was in school, but that's in the past. It's now my responsibility to teach it and I'm going to give it my best shot. I reviewed the lesson plans Mrs. Higgins gave me for class. My first task was to distribute the math test that Mrs. Higgins graded the night before. My instructions to the students were as follows. "When I call your name, come to the front desk to get your test." When distributing each test I noticed that all students received passing grades except for one student, Charles, who failed.

After all the tests were distributed I noticed the students were talking amongst each other about the test and were telling each other the grade they achieved.

While the class was talking, I was busy writing various math equations and word problems (boy, do I hate word problems) on the white board that was part of the day's lesson. While writing the problems on the board I overheard one of the students (Paul) asking Charlie what grade he got on the test. Charlie didn't answer. Paul asked him again and Charlie still didn't answer. Suddenly, Paul grabbed the test from Charlie's desk and saw his grade; it was a 59. Immediately, upon seeing the grade, Paul began shouting, "Charlie failed the test, Charlie failed the test!"

When the class heard that Charlie failed, they all started to laugh and make fun of him. When I looked at Charlie, the disappointment and embarrassment in his eyes spoke volumes.

Immediately, I shouted angrily. "Stop talking this instant! You should all be ashamed of yourselves. Raise your hand if you never failed a test." I waited a moment and then continued. "I see that no one raised his or her hand. Apparently, everyone has failed a test. I have another question. How would you feel if a teacher or student singled you out and announced to the whole class that you failed a test? I'm sure you wouldn't have liked it. I'm very disappointed in your behavior. This is an eighth grade class, you should know better. I want you all to apologize to Charlie. You all acted like a bunch of bullies."

After class I told Charlie to see me. I asked, "Charlie, are you okay?"

"Yes," said Charlie.

I said, "You know Charlie, the students that made fun of you today were wrong. Don't let them bother you. You saw their reaction when I said 'Raise your hand if you never failed a test.' Nobody raised his or her hand."

"Thank you for that, Mr. Minnow," said Charlie. "When I saw that no one raised their hand I felt better."

I replied, "I know you will pass your next test."

Charlie said, "Yes, I'm confident I will pass the next test. I reviewed the test and I know I made careless mistakes. I realize what I did wrong. It won't happen again."

I said, "Way to go, Charlie, I like your attitude." After we spoke, Charlie went to his next class.

A few weeks later, a similar incident occurred. I was subbing for a history teacher this time. The lesson was about the Civil War. I asked the class a variety of questions and the students responded with answers.

I asked the first question. "What was the name of the general of the North?"

A boy raised his hand and said, "General Lee."

Before I could correct him, one of the students (Paul) shouted, "Wrong answer, stupid!"

Immediately, I shouted back. "Paul, you are way out of line. You are being very disrespectful. I will not allow rude behavior in the classroom."

After reprimanding Paul, I moved on to the next question. "What was the name given to the army of the North?"

Another student raised their hand and answered, "The Confederate Army."

Again, Paul shouted, "Wrong answer! Your answer is as stupid as the last one."

Angrily, I said, "Paul, didn't you listen to what I just told you? Get up this instant and go to guidance. I will not tolerate this type of behavior. Bullying is not allowed in this school. I will call guidance to let them know to expect you. Obviously you have not learned how to respect your classmates."

Later, I received a call from guidance stating Paul received a detention.

My hope was the class would understand how wrong it is to bully someone and that the fact Paul received a detention for behaving like a bully, would emphasize that bullying will not be tolerated.

About a week later, I received a call to substitute teach for an English class. Students were entering the classroom and were getting settled in their seats. I was busy reviewing that day's lesson plan, when suddenly I heard a loud thumping noise. When I looked up, I saw one of the students (Jake) sprawled out on the floor. Seeing

Jake fall, most of the students began to laugh uncontrollably. I asked the class, "What happened?" No one responded. I then said, "If I don't get an answer, I'll make sure the entire class stays after school for detention."

After a few minutes of silence, Jake stood up and said, "I was going to sit down when Ted pulled the chair out from under me."

I turned to Ted and asked, "Did you pull the chair away from Jake?"

"Yes," said Ted.

I promptly replied, "Why did you do that?"

Ted said with a smirk on his face, "I was just having some fun."

I replied firmly, "That's not having fun. What you did was cruel and insensitive and Jake could've been hurt. You acted like a bully. As I strongly stated before, I will not tolerate bully behavior in class.

I spoke to the principal about bullying and he told me to send any students who bully other students to his office. Ted, please collect your books and go to the principal's office."

At the end of class, the principal called me and said he contacted Ted's parents and Ted will be punished. I wondered, *would Ted ever learn his lesson that it's wrong to bully people?*

As a substitute teacher, I realized that some students are bullies. I also realized that students often fail to stay on task and are easily distracted. For example, in class, students would fool around with friends, play games on their computer, stare at the clock, look out the window and routinely not pay attention.

Then, it hit me.

I behaved exactly the same way when I was in school. Although there were no computers, I too was easily distracted and fooled around with my friends. I realized something else, something important. I judged my teachers unfairly, especially Sister Superior. As I reflect back to my 13-year-old self, I misjudged and exaggerated the actions of Sister Superior. Sister really wasn't so bad or mean-spirited. There was a very good reason why she acted the way she did. She had to be strict for our own good. It was the only way she could get us to stay focused on our studies. I know that now, more than ever. I then thought to myself, '*A big thank you to my teachers, especially Sister Superior. You helped mold me into the person I am today.*'

After drifting back into reality, I prepared a short quiz. It won't take you long to complete the quiz and you don't have to worry about it being graded.

Here's the quiz. Read the following statements below. Determine which statements are true and which are false. I will give you the answers at the end.

- ❖ **Friends are never bullies. (T or F)**
- ❖ **Bullies will go away if you ignore them. (T or F)**
- ❖ **Bullies often change their behavior. (T or F)**
- ❖ **The best way to deal with bullies is to fight back. (T or F)**
- ❖ **People should mind their own business if they see someone being bullied. (T or F)**

❖ You are a tattletale if you tell an adult you are being bullied. (T or F)

❖ Abusive teasing is not bullying. (T or F)

❖ You are not a bully unless you physically hurt someone. (T or F)

❖ If you tell someone you are being bullied, you are a crybaby. (T or F)

❖ If someone bullies you, it's okay to bully him or her back. (T or F)

You may have figured this out by now. The answers to all of the statements of the quiz are 100 percent false. Totally not true. Congratulations to everyone who answered correctly.

15

My Big and Shocking Surprise

W ell, another school day has ended and I just got home. The first thing I do is to check my computer to see if I received any emails or Facebook notifications.

My big and shocking surprise…

Remember Xavier Steele (alias Xman), the boy who bullied me in ninth grade? Well, something astonishing happened. Xman found me on Facebook and said he wanted to meet with me, but that wasn't the astonishing part. **I'll explain...**

About a week later we met at Starbucks. When I walked into Starbucks I saw Xman sitting next to the window. Although he looked much older, I recognized him immediately. I looked older too and he recognized me as well. I said, "Xavier (I didn't want to call him Xman), what's it been thirty years? It's great to see you."

Xavier replied, "It's great to see you too." After we reminisced for a while, Xavier suddenly became very serious. His facial expression changed; there was a sincere and vulnerable look on his face. He said, "Joseph, I wanted to meet with you today to personally apologize for bullying you in school. You may find this hard to believe, but my bad behavior in school, particularly against you, has been haunting me for all these years. I realize I was young at the time, but there is no excuse for my bad behavior. I'm so ashamed I acted that way. My bad behavior affected me psychologically, so much in fact that I had to see a psychiatrist for help and treatment. The psychiatrist told me in order to free myself from my guilt I must apologize to you in person, which is why it was so important for me to meet with you today. So, Joseph, I'm so sorry for bullying you in school. I realize how wrong I was to bully you. I have been hurting for many years. Can you find it in your heart to forgive me?"

I looked at Xavier, his glassy eyes narrowed. I said, "Yes, absolutely. I forgive you 100 percent. Do me a favor and free yourself from this guilt. We all make mistakes in life; I've made my share. It's important to forgive and I forgive you."

Xavier remained silent for a minute. For a moment it seemed like he was holding his breath; then, he slowly let out a deep sigh. It looked as if a great weight was lifted from his shoulders. He looked at me and smiled. This was no ordinary smile; it had the look of appreciation and relief. It was the type of smile that was unattainable for many years. If a smile could speak, it would shout out sheer delight. He shook my hand and as he was walking away he said, "Joseph, remember Bob Booker. I replied, "Sure, how could I ever forget BB." Xavier said, "He is the mayor of his town." I just stared in disbelief. After that day, I never heard from Xavier again.

Could you imagine that being a bully all those years ago could have such a powerful impact on a person later on in life? I'm happy Xavier is now at peace with himself.

I received another big surprise, but this time it was not good. One morning I was reading the newspaper when I came across another familiar name from school. It was Butch Barotti. The article said Butch was convicted of armed robbery and sentenced to prison for ten years.

I was sorry to read that Butch was in prison. You never want to see something like that happen to anyone, especially someone you know. I guess if you are a bully early in life, it can sometimes lead a person to commit a criminal act later on in life. How very sad.

16

The Cyberbully

It seems like nothing can escape the bad behavior of a bully: whenever a new aven ue presents itself, a bully will find a way to use it to their advantage; the latest is ***Social Media.*** The internet created a new kind of bully – the **Cyberbully**.

There is no question social media has had a major impact on all our lives. This impact has been mostly beneficial and positive. However, as with most things in life, there is good and bad. Sometimes the bad can be very bad, with devastating consequences.

Since I'm the eternal optimist, I will start with the good. To that end, with social media you can...

Stay in touch with relatives and friends, conduct job searches, access the latest news in real time, provide or receive personal advice, counteract crime or perhaps terrorism, access a vast amount of information including educational, financial, and medical, etc.; help charities deliver their needs to help people, promote products and services, listen to music or watch a video and on and on. The good points are endless.

Now for the bad. One of the biggest negatives of social media can be summed up in one word —

"CYBERBULLYING"

Discouragingly, social media can also bring out the worst in people. It's another avenue bullies can use to harass people and negatively impact a person's dignity and pride. Cyberbullying can be used to:

Spread lies, secrets, gossip and rumors;
Post embarrassing or hurtful pictures and images;
Create blogs or websites with stories or jokes ridiculing others;
Threaten and harass people;
Conduct identity theft;
Reveal personal and private information;
Steal financial data;
Conduct various acts of internet crime;
Promote terrorism
and on and on.

This is just the tip of the iceberg. The effects of cyberbullying are in many ways worse than traditional bullying, infiltrating every part of a victim's life and causing psychological struggles. There are so many different ways social media can be used to hurt people. Fooling around and making cruel and insensitive comments with friends in person may have very little impact; however, posting the same information online or posting harmful or embarrassing text or inappropriate photos can damage a reputation and cause problems years later. It is a permanent record that may never go away.

So what can you do, if you are the originator of these online messages?

It's really quite simple: use the intelligence that God gave you. Think carefully before you post anything online. If you are not sure whether to post it or not, err on the side of caution and don't post it. It's similar to what my mom told me many years ago: if you can't say something nice or you are not sure if it's nice, don't say it.

Another way to determine whether or not you should post text or pictures online is to ask yourself this question:

"Will someone find this post hurtful in any way?" If the answer is yes, '**DO NOT POST IT**'.

Once again my daughter was a victim. One day, Emma came home from school extremely upset. As soon as she came into the house, she ran up to her room crying. Seeing Emma crying, my wife went up to talk with her. Later that evening, my wife told me what had happened. She said Emma told her she was cyberbullied. She continued and said Emma was invited to Nicole's party, one of her good friends. At the party one of the girls (Alice), a well-known troublemaker, used her cell phone to take a picture of Emma while she was holding a glass of soda. After the party, Alice posted the picture on Facebook with the message, "Check out Emma, drinking heavily at Alice's party. By the time the party was over, Emma was out of her mind drunk."

The next day at school, everyone was talking about the picture of Emma on Facebook. All day at school, people were teasing her about the picture. This went on for several days. Emma replied to everyone who teased her that she only drank soda at the party and was never drunk.

Later, Emma confronted Alice, asking her why she would do such a thing. Alice, seemingly not caring, nonchalantly said, "I was just having some fun. Only kidding."

Emma said in an aggravated tone, "This is not just having fun. It was cruel and hurtful."

Alice said, with no remorse, "You're overreacting. Grow up."

As the day went on, other girls who attended the party came to Emma's defense. They told everyone at school Emma was only drinking soda and that Alice completely made up the story about Emma being drunk. It was all one big lie. Although the truth came out and everyone knew Emma wasn't drinking alcohol at the party, Emma remained upset for weeks.

Emma wasn't the only person in school to experience cyberbullying; other people she knew were also bullied. One of her friends, Rosa, was deeply hurt because she was cyberbullied.

Lately, Rosa's parents were constantly arguing with each other. When Rosa was lying in bed trying to fall asleep, she would hear her parents yelling and screaming at each other. This went on for weeks and weeks. One night, while her parents were fighting, Rosa couldn't take it anymore and felt she had to talk to someone. Looking for someone to comfort her, she decided to email her friend Ellie. Her email contained detailed information about what her parents were fighting about. She said her parents were calling each other bad names, cruel and insensitive names and used profanity. She said her parents spoke about separating and getting a divorce. They fought over who would take care of Rosa.

Rosa was looking to Ellie for emotional support. However, instead of sending an email response only to Rosa, Ellie forwarded the email to ten other girls.

Regrettably, Rosa started to receive emails from all the other girls. Rosa was never friendly with these girls and hardly knew them. Rosa was horrified to learn that her friend Ellie, whom she confided in, had betrayed her trust. The email responses contained very insensitive and insulting remarks, such as:

- ❖ If I was a parent and had a daughter as ugly as you, I would also want to get a divorce.
- ❖ You are the only reason your parents are getting a divorce, because you are a total mess.

❖ Everyone knows you're not doing well in school; you are an embarrassment to your parents. They're probably arguing about how much of a burden you are to them.

Rosa continued to receive cruel email messages. As a result, the messages actually made her sick. She became so upset that she ended up missing days at school. She was so emotionally shaken she was put under a doctor's care and was treated for depression.

Eventually, Rosa felt better. However, it took her a very long time to recover from depression. The mental anguish caused her much suffering.

After hearing Rosa's story, Dakota, who was friends with Rosa, told her about her experience with a cyberbully. Dakota explained she was on MySpace with a group of friends. One day, Dakota had a heated argument with Amy, one of the girls in the group. As a result of the argument, Amy created a fake MySpace profile. The fake profile contained a variety of pictures, which made Dakota look extremely ugly. Apparently, Amy used Photoshop to alter Dakota's hair to make it look uncombed and disheveled. She made Dakota's face appear distorted and covered with acne.

Furthermore, the fake MySpace profile contained Dakota's cell phone number and email address.

It didn't take long before Dakota was getting calls and email from strangers who would call her names and make fun of her. The texting, calls and email got so bad, she started to believe she was unattractive and that nobody liked her.

Dakota never told her mom what happened. Her mom, as all moms do, noticed Dakota looked very sad and depressed almost every day. Finally, her mom sat her down and pleaded with her to tell her what was wrong. Still, Dakota didn't say a word. Eventually, her mom was really worried and began to think Dakota was in some kind of trouble; then, she just broke down and cried. After seeing her mother so upset and crying, Dakota told her about MySpace and why she's been so unhappy. Her mom said, "I know just what to do." She was a mom on a mission. There is no power on earth more powerful than the power of a mom on a mission.

First, Dakota's mom helped her daughter delete all known online presence and proceeded to change her cell phone number, as well as her email address. After the changes were made, a remarkable thing happened; Dakota felt she had a new lease on life. Her mom changed as well. She started to spend more time with Dakota and would routinely compliment her, when she never did before.

Each day her mom would say wonderful things about her daughter. She made comments like Dakota was special in many ways, that she was smart, worked hard and had the talent to achieve great things.

It's ironic how a bad experience can sometimes bring people closer together. Dakota's mom was now spending much more time with her, taking her shopping, helping her with her homework and just listening and talking to her more intently. Yes, Dakota and her mom were not only mother and daughter, but were now best friends as well, all of which happened after Dakota was cyberbullied.

Another one of Emma's girlfriends (Jesse) called her to speak about her cyberbully experience. This time it didn't involve Jesse; instead, it was Jesse's brother Dave. Jesse told Emma, "What a cyberbully did to my brother was not only cruel, it was deeply disturbing and embarrassing." Jesse paused for a moment, struggling to find the right words. "It's so disgusting, it is hard for me to talk about it. I feel it's important for me to tell you, though, because of what you've been through. My brother was in the boy's bathroom at school using the urinal. There was another boy in the bathroom on his cell phone, texting his friends. His name was Brad. My brother was never a friend of Brad's, but he knew of him from school. While my brother was standing at the urinal, he failed to notice that Brad took pictures of him with his cell phone. Then, a terrible thing happened. Brad posted the pictures on the internet. My brother was in school when people started making fun of him. They were calling him names and making rude comments, giggling and telling jokes. They called him Mr. Wee Wee, Brad Pee Pee, Mr. Tinkleman, Captain Spritz and other terrible names. Kids in school were relentless; the insults were nonstop. For a while, my brother didn't know the reason why people were making fun of him. Finally, one of his friends showed him the pictures that were posted. After seeing the pictures, my brother was deeply hurt and embarrassed. He couldn't believe someone would do something so cruel and insensitive."

Emma was shocked. She couldn't believe someone could do such a thing. Jesse continued. "My brother told my parents what had happened. My father called the police and eventually pressed charges. We don't know what the outcome will be, but I'm proud of my brother for speaking up. He could have kept quiet; instead, he did the right thing by telling my parents."

Jesse then said, "My sincere hope is that my brother's action will prevent Brad and people like him from cyberbullying someone else."

Another incident happened to Kiara. She is a student in my daughter's class, who unfortunately was also a cyberbully victim.

There were a few girls that were part of a circle of friends. The girls were mean-spirited, obnoxious, loved to gossip, tell lies and make fun of people. Simply put, they just weren't nice.

Two girls, for no reason, started to harass Kiara. The girls were active on all of the popular social media sites such as Facebook, Snapchat, Instagram, Twitter, MySpace, etc. They called themselves the "The Cyber Girls".

The Cyber Girls

Kiara was overweight her entire life. She tried different diets to lose weight, but never achieved success. The Cyber Girls were thin, pretty and popular. Inexplicably, they decided to team up and bully Kiara about her weight. Kiara was never friends with any member of the Cyber Girls; in fact, she never spoke to any of them.

The Cyber Girls began sending Kiara mean-spirited emails stating, "How does it feel being a fat ugly pig with no friends? You are too big to call yourself plus size. You will go through your whole worthless life being fat and overweight. Your weight is so disgusting it makes me sick just looking at you."

After reading the emails, Kiara became very depressed. She didn't understand why girls she hardly knew would send her such horrible emails. Kiara tried her best to ignore them, but the emails kept coming.

There was one thing Kiara loved immensely, her dog Happy, a toy poodle. Kiara would spend hours playing with Happy. Kiara would tell everyone how much she loved her dog. When Kiara was sad or upset, she would look to her dog for comfort. She would spend quality time with Happy, which for a while helped her forget about the insensitive and cruel messages.

The Cyber Girls discovered how much Kiara loved her dog and they started to include the dog as part of their cyber bashing. One tweet said, "We hate you and your stupid dog. We know where you walk your dog and one night when you least expect it, we're going to sneak up on you and kill your dog. We also know you let your dog run free in your backyard. Be careful, maybe someone will poison a piece of meat and throw it over the fence. Your dog is too stupid to know the meat is poisoned and will eat it and die."

The Cyber Girls also used Snapchat to harass people. Kiara made sure to block the Cyber Girls so they wouldn't see photos/pictures Kiara posted. Unfortunately, that didn't stop them. The Cyber Girls were able to look at Kiara 's Snapchat posts on other girls' phones and then use Snapchat to send threatening and insulting messages back to Kiara.

As time went on, the threats became more and more intense and worrisome. The text messages suggested the girls were going to gang up on Kiara and beat her up. One message said, "Your locker is going to be vandalized."

One week after Kiara received the threatening messages, her locker was broken into and all of her personal belongings were stolen.

The next attack came quickly; the Cyber Girls began to spread vicious lies and rumors. One of the text messages accused Kiara of being a racist. Kiara was not a racist; quite the contrary, she supported diversity and had African-American friends. However, the girls made up the story with the intention of proving she was a racist. It was all one big lie.

The threatening messages continued for weeks and weeks. Finally, Kiara couldn't take it anymore. She was at her wits end and told her mother.

Her mom was devastated to hear such dreadful news and realized how much Kiara was suffering.

Prior to hearing Kiara's story, her mom had noticed Kiara was often depressed and was suffering from anxiety attacks. Her mom just thought Kiara was going through a phase, that it was just part of growing up and adjusting to school. She had no idea the reason Kiara felt this way was the result of being cyberbullied.

Kiara's mom told her daughter she would do everything in her power to put a stop to this bad behavior.

The first thing Kiara's mom did was call the parents of each Cyber Girl. Regrettably, this action did not resolve the problem because The Cyber Girls denied the whole thing. They said Kiara was overreacting and exaggerated her story. Unfortunately, the girls' parents believed their daughters, so the parents did nothing to stop their daughters' bad behavior.

Kiara's mom then contacted the school. The principal said he would speak to the girls and resolve the problem. As promised, the principal discussed the issue with each girl, but to no avail. Again, the girls denied everything and even worse, continued to bully Kiara.

Kiara's mother took other action as well, but nothing seemed to work.

Unfortunately, this story does not have a happy ending.

A month later, Kiara decided it would be best to change schools. Kiara liked the school and had some really good friends, but she believed she had no choice. In order to escape from being bullied, she had to leave school. She was just tired of being the victim.

What a sad and terrible ending to this story.

17

What Is Bullying

Often, you hear people say, I didn't realize I was bullying or I was just teasing or fooling around. I didn't mean to bully anyone. I strongly disagree with these statements. I believe people, deep down in their hearts, know the difference between harmless teasing and actual bullying. It's not that hard to figure out. Statements similar to the ones above are just plain excuses made by bullies trying to justify their bad behavior.

As I think back, I remember Father Timothy's definition of a bully. I was curious to see if today's definition of bullying had changed. So, where's the best place to find the definition? The internet, of course.

Wikipedia defines bullying as "the use of force, threat, or coercion to abuse, intimidate, or aggressively dominate others. The behavior is often repeated and habitual. One essential prerequisite is the perception, by the bully or by others of an imbalance of social or physical power, which distinguishes bullying from conflict. Behaviors used to assert such domination can include verbal harassment or threat, physical assault or coercion and such acts may be directed repeatedly towards particular targets. Rationalizations of such behavior sometimes include difference in social class, race, religion, gender, sexual orientation, appearance, lineage, strength, size or ability. If bullying is done in a group, it is called mobbing."

Bullying can be defined in many different ways in the United States and other countries. The United Kingdom of Great Britain and Northern Ireland have no legal definition of bullying; however, some states in the United States have laws against it. Bullying is divided into four basic types of abuse:

- ❖ **Emotional**
- ❖ **Verbal**
- ❖ **Physical**
- ❖ **Property Damage**

Bullying typically involves subtle methods of coercion, such as intimidation. Bullying ranges from one-on-one individual bullying through to group bullying, in which there are "lieutenants", who may seem to be willing to assist the primary bully in his or her bullying activities. Bullying in school and the workplace is also referred to as peer abuse.

A bullying culture can develop in any context in which humans interact with each other. This includes school, the workplace, at home, in a shopping mall, restaurants, anywhere.

There are two approaches to bullying:

❖ **Direct**
❖ **Indirect**

Direct is against a person or group. Indirect is not directed at a person, but indirectly such as spreading lies and rumors.

I believe the Wikipedia definition failed to include an important aspect about bullying—*"the intensity level"*. A bully's intensity level can vary greatly. For example, the intensity level is at its highest when a bully physically hurts their victim or loudly screams out a verbal attack against someone. This extreme violent action can lead to serious depression, anxiety and in some cases, suicide.

When people witness this bad behavior at its highest level, bullying is easily recognized. However, it's important to note that even at its lowest level of intensity, bullying is still bullying.

When a person's primary intent is to ridicule, embarrass or physically hurt someone, *even in the slightest way*, this is bullying.

The bully may think their actions are no big deal, but in fact, it is a big deal.

In the mind of a bully, their bad behavior may seem innocent or trivial, but make no mistake, anytime a person takes delight in seeing their victim in pain, no matter how small the pain, it is bullying. So, when someone makes fun of a person's glasses, their clothes, their braces, the way they talk, their looks, etc. (you get the point) and does so with the intent to make that person feel bad, it is bullying.

I've provided the Wikipedia definition of bullying.

Now, I give you my own definition:

Simply stated, "Bullying is when someone physically or emotionally threatens, hurts or abuses you or damages your property, with the mindset to intentionally do so. When a person is bullied, even in the slightest way, it is still bullying. Bullying is bullying no matter the level of severity."

18

Bully Statistics

Bullying has now reached epidemic proportions. Incidents of people being bullied continue to rise year after year. More people, especially children and teens, are victims of being bullied. Bullying usually occurs in schools or is school related, but unfortunately has no boundaries and can occur anywhere at any time including home, work, shopping, parking a car, anywhere.

School bullying statistics indicate that about **13 million** school children in the U.S. are victims of bullying and that **1 in 4 children** are bullied regularly on school grounds. This statistic illustrates how prevalent bullying is in our schools and how grave a problem bullying has become.

Of the students that reported being bullied in the National Crime Victimization Survey [NCES, 2013] —

❖ 64.5 percent said it was once or twice in the school year
❖ 18.5 percent said once or twice a month
❖ 9.2 percent said once or twice a week
❖ 7.8 percent said almost every day

According to a recent SAFE Survey (2010), the most likely group to be affected regarding school bullying is young people in **grades 6 through 10.**

In a recent article (Anatomy of School Bullying by Stephan Merrill), bullying occurs more frequently depending on the location. While a school's playground usually records the highest incidents of bully behavior, it's the more transitional areas, the fast moving, highly social hallways and stairways that dominate the landscape of school harassment.

Almost 42 percent of students who were bullied reported incidents in hallways and stairways, a number that was similar for boys (41.8 percent) and girls (41.6 percent). A small percentage of bullied students reported incidents outside the school grounds (19.3 percent), in the bathroom or locker rooms (9.4 percent), in the school cafeteria (22.2 percent) or on a school bus (10 percent).

It is reported in the CDC Youth Risk Behavior Survey (2013 report) that on average across 39 states surveyed, 7.2 percent of students admit to not going to school due to personal safety concerns. The statistics are staggering. Up to **160,000** children stay home from school every day because they are afraid they will be bullied.

Can you imagine that so many students are not going to school because they are being bullied? In many cases these students don't tell their parents the actual reason why they are not going to school. Often they make excuses like they don't feel well or pretend they are going to school, but actually go somewhere else instead. So, bullying can result in children lying to their parents, where under normal circumstances they would never lie.

Many dread the physical and verbal aggression of their peers and many more attend school in a chronic state of anxiety and depression. It's reported that 70.6 percent of young people say they have seen bullying in their schools. While bullying can result in reluctance to go to school, other negative effects include headaches, stomach pains, reduced appetite, shame, anxiety, irritability, aggression, depression and suicide.

Social media is the latest vehicle used to bully people. At least 52 percent of teens have been bullied online according to iSafe Foundation [2014]. Cyberbullying includes being bullied through email, chat rooms, instant messaging, websites or texting.

One million children on Facebook alone were harassed in 2011 as reported by Consumer Reports.

DoSomething.org suggests that 90 percent of children in grades 4 through 8 have been bullied at some point in their young lives.

The sheer number of children and young adults that are being bullied is appalling to me, as are the consequences of being bullied, like missing school, feeling sick, depressed and in some cases committing suicide.

For the bullies themselves, studies show their bully mentality can stay with them throughout their entire life and sometimes can lead them to abuse their spouse, their children, friends and co-workers. In some cases, a bully's mindset can cause them to resort to gun violence and crime.

What do all these statistics tell us?

"We must all work hard to end this epidemic. Bullying must be stopped."

19

Why Do People Bully

Since bullies have victimized me, I often wonder why people bully other people. Is being a bully something we are born with, some sort of bad inherited human instinct? Is it part of a person's DNA? If it is something we are born with or inherited, why isn't everyone a bully or at least start out his or her lives as bullies?

What kind of pleasure or satisfaction does one get from being a bully? Since being a bully is so appalling to me, something I would never do, it's difficult for me to understand why so many people are bullies.

Yet the reality is, there are many people who are bullies and the numbers are growing. Whatever the reason, bullying is thriving and continues to rise.

If we can determine the reason why people bully, maybe we can take the necessary steps to prevent it or reduce the frequency.

Some people believe bullying is just a phase some kids go through, that it's part of growing up and it's no big deal. Emphatically, I say, this is the absolute wrong way to think. This kind of thinking helps fuel the problem, not help reduce it.

I've heard some people say, "Maybe there was a reason the person was bullied." Again, emphatically I say, "There is never a good reason to bully someone. It can never be justified."

This begs the question, **"Why do people bully?"**

TheHopeline.com reports there are many reasons why people bully. People may see it as a way to be in control over friends and relatives. Others may bully because they believe it makes them feel popular or think others find it funny. Some bully for the sole purpose of getting attention. It could also be they are jealous of the person they're bullying. They may be getting bullied themselves and bully others they perceive as weaker. These are just a few reasons, but unfortunately there are many more.

Here is more detailed information on why people bully:

~BULLIES ARE INSECURE~

Some people are bullies because they are insecure. On the outside they may appear strong and in control, but from the inside feel insecure, inferior and have low self-esteem. To make matters worse, they often believe their parents/guardians, relatives and friends see themselves as inferior. This emotional distress may cause the person to take out their frustrations by bullying others as a way to boost their own self-esteem. Since bullies feel insecure, they try to create the perception of being in control by bullying others who appear to be weak and vulnerable, whom they believe are easy targets. Typically, these are people, who in the mind of the bully, are timid and defenseless and can be easily overpowered.

In some cases, the unthinkable happens; people that have physical or emotional disabilities are targeted. This is why I believe most bullies who are insecure are cowards as well. They victimize people who are ill equipped to defend themselves. You rarely see a bully attack a person bigger and stronger than they are. They make sure that they target the weak and defenseless. How very sad.

~BULLIES ARE JEALOUS~

Some people become bullies because they are jealous of other people. If a bully is jealous of a particular person, they'll take out their frustrations on that person. They may be jealous of a person's looks, financial status, special talents, athletic ability, relationships with others, the reasons are endless.

The main reason for jealousy is often popularity. When a bully realizes a person is more popular than they are, the bully may lash out against him/her and bully them simply because they are more popular.

Bullies sometimes are jealous of a person's individual interest or skill. For example, a person who is a member of the chess club may be targeted because the bully cannot play chess or is not a good chess player or the bully is jealous of the person who always gets the highest grade in class, etc.

~BULLIES SEEK POWER~

Bullies often pick on people they think they can have power over. They bully people who are weak; whom they know won't fight back. They gain a sense of power by intimidation using physical force or psychologically with verbal abuse. Getting a big reaction out of someone can make bullies feel like they have the power they want. They pick on kids who get easily upset. Bullies seeking power attempt to strike fear in their victims by threatening or embarrassing them.

Some of the ways bullies physically exert power against their victims include pushing, spitting, punching, kicking and throwing objects at them. Regrettably, there are countless ways bullies physically hurt their victims.

Bullies can also hurt people verbally by threats, calling them names, spreading rumors, taunting, using abusive language and through humiliation. They verbally abuse people by attacking their physical appearance (short, skinny, overweight, bad complexion, etc.), how they dress, their race, religious beliefs and sexual orientation.

~BULLIES LOOK FOR ATTENTION~

In some cases, bullies are very lonely, do not have a meaningful social life and have few or no true friends. Since they cannot make friends the proper way, they bully others to get the attention they desperately need. These people are often socially awkward and feel disconnected from people. These social issues lead them to have trouble communicating in a healthy way and instead turn to insults or physical violence as a way to communicate. Unfortunately, in their mind, bullying is the only action they believe they can use to get the attention they crave.

~BULLIES HAVE FAMILY ISSUES~

Some bullies come from families where everyone is angry and shouting all the time and are not warm and loving. They come from homes where there is a lack of understanding and sensitivity towards one another. These families are dysfunctional in many ways. Parents/guardians often fail to provide for many of their children's emotional and physical needs. In this type of environment, family members do not respect each other and are often inconsiderate and mean-spirited. Children may witness their parents/guardians being aggressive, disrespectful and uncaring towards friends and other family members or may witness parents/guardians having marital or relationship issues. Often, there is a lack of quality time family members spend together causing families to drift apart. Children may experience a constant feeling of loneliness and depression.

Children may be exposed to violence at home, which can lead to violence outside the home.

Individuals who grow up in this type of dysfunctional environment can become frustrated due to the way they are treated and often take out their frustration by bullying others.

~BULLIES WHO ARE BULLIED THEMSELVES~

A person that is being bullied by his parents, siblings or friends may respond negatively by becoming bullies themselves. Instead of reaching out for help, their anger and frustration leads them down the wrong path—the path of becoming a bully.

You might think the opposite would be true. When a person is bullied, they are hurt and offended and should realize how it feels to be a victim, and not want to be a bully themselves. Regrettably, in some cases, the reaction is that of retaliation, but not against the person who bullied them, but against anyone.

Conclusion

As you can see, the reason people bully is complex and influenced by many factors. It is impossible to list every reason, so my goal is to touch upon the more common ones. I'm sure there are many more reasons you can think of yourself.

Regardless of the reason, it's important to note, ***there is never a good or valid reason for one person to bully another person. No one, no matter what the circumstance, deserves to be bullied. Bullying can never be justified. NEVER!***

20

What To Do When Bullied

If there is only one thing you learn from reading this book, just one takeaway, it is two simple words:

"SAY SOMETHING"

Don't be like me when I was in school. I allowed Butch Barotti and Xavier Steele to bully me. I said nothing and did nothing to stop it. I had to learn the hard way. I said nothing for a very long time and suffered for it. More importantly, I let other people suffer on my account. Since I refused to speak up, the person that bullied me also bullied my friends and others. I had plenty of chances to say something. My friends and teachers encouraged me to speak up, but I wouldn't listen.

People say you are squealing or acting like a coward for speaking up about being bullied. Nothing could be further from the truth. In fact, the opposite is true. By speaking up you are standing up for yourself and making the statement: this type of behavior is wrong and will not be tolerated. This is an act of bravery, not cowardice.

There were numerous reasons why I didn't want to speak up. Some of my reasons were:

- ❖ I was afraid the bully would find out and become more aggressive towards me.
- ❖ I thought the bully would start bullying my friends.
- ❖ I thought everyone would say I'm a squealer.
- ❖ I thought if I said nothing, keeping a low profile, the bully would just forget about me and go away.

I finally realized that none of these reasons were valid, just excuses; the bullies didn't go away; instead, they continued to bully me.

You may feel helpless, afraid and alone when dealing with bullies. You may think the situation is hopeless and there's nothing you can do about it. However, this is the **WRONG** way to think. You may be surprised to know there are a number of things you can do to stop an individual or group from bullying you.

So, the million-dollar question is, **"What do you do if you are bullied?"** I have the answer. You can —

"SAY SOMETHING"

I said it before and I'll say it again — ***say something***. ***Don't keep it a secret.*** I'm not just asking you, I'm begging you. "***Please say something!***" It's the best way to get help from being bullied.

This is the most important action item you could do to stop a bully. You may ask, "Who could I ask for help?" The answer is quite simple. Ask a person you trust.

You should have plenty of people to choose from. You can speak with a parent, brother or sister, a relative, friend, teacher, guidance counselor, school nurse, coach, a member of the school's office staff and the list goes on. It doesn't matter who you choose, just make sure you speak with someone.

Typically, a bully will not go away if you ignore them, which is why it is so important to say something/do something. Remember, you are not squealing or tattling when someone is verbally or physically abusing you. Additionally, by telling someone you may help prevent someone else from being bullied. No person under any circumstance deserves to be bullied.

If you speak with someone and you feel that person is not taking you seriously or not listening to you, don't give up; speak with someone else.

As previously mentioned, the best way to stop a bully is to tell someone. Here are other suggestions to stop someone from bullying you...

~Travel in a Group~

Bullies especially target people who are alone. A bully believes a person alone is vulnerable and an easy target. If at all possible, avoid being alone with bullies. To help avoid being bullied, make a conscious effort to hang out in a group, ideally with a group of friends. When people surround you, a bully is less likely to single you out and pick on you. Consider asking a friend or group of friends to meet you at your classroom when the bell rings, so you don't have to walk alone. Find ways to travel more often with someone you trust. Simply put, if you travel in a group, you are less likely to be bullied. There is a reason the smallest fish in the sea congregate in large numbers. There is truth to the saying, "There is strength and safety in numbers."

~Don't Fight Back/Use Diplomacy~

Often bullies are looking for a fight. It's tempting to want to fight back, but don't do it. Again, don't be like me when I was in school. This is exactly what a bully is attempting to do, get you to fight back. Do not respond with aggression, try your best to avoid confrontation; instead, act as if you don't care. If you ignore a bully, they often get frustrated and will refrain from bullying you. More importantly, you don't want to lower yourself to the mindset of a bully or God forbid become a bully yourself. Remember that fighting is seldom the answer and escalating the situation can be dangerous and may result in injury to you and/or the bully. Instead of using physical strength, use your inner strength and try to reason with the bully. Diplomacy can sometimes diffuse the situation. Be assertive; demonstrate you can stand up for yourself.

In a clear, calm, but decisive voice, tell the bully to stop. Explain you don't want trouble, but you don't like their behavior. Try your best to exude confidence. Look the bully in the eye and with body language show him/her "a don't mess with me attitude."

Another reason not to fight back is that you may get into trouble yourself; so fighting back is never a good idea.

If a bully refuses to back down, just walk away. If you feel it's necessary, walk directly to a teacher, the principal or someone you believe can help you and explain what happened.

~Avoid Bullies Whenever Possible~

This may sound obvious, but simply avoid places where the bully is likely to be. Typically, you know the people who are the bullies in the school. When possible, try your best to avoid them or the areas where they hang out. If you know they congregate in certain areas of the school such as in front of a specific vending machine, water fountain, bathroom, certain sections of the hallway, at their locker, same table in the cafeteria, etc., avoid those areas. Pay attention to your surroundings. If a bully approaches you, **walk away**. Walking away doesn't mean you are afraid. Quite the contrary, it takes courage to just walk away.

If you keep your distance from bullies, you can avoid being seen and avoid being bullied. "Out of sight, out of mind."

Don't spend a lot of time hanging out by your locker. Bullies target these areas, so quickly remove your books from your locker and hurry on your way. Think of ways to change or alter your normal routine. For example, find a new way to walk home from school, ask friends to walk home with you or leave at a different time. Occasionally, make arrangements with a parent/guardian to pick you up. Sometimes, little changes can make a big difference.

~Send an Email~

Some people who are bullied find it difficult to speak with someone in person. There is another option—send an email.

It's important to note that before you send your email, be careful to accurately record each event. Write a detailed account of what happened. Record the bully's name, your name, the time and place of each incident, exactly what happened and photographs of injury to yourself or your property, if applicable. The more detail the better. Send the email to someone you can trust, someone you believe is the best person who can help you.

~Ask If Your School Has an Anti-Bullying Policy~

Some schools have anti-bullying policies specifically created to help stop or prevent bullying. Speak with a teacher and ask if your school has an anti-bullying policy. Some schools appoint an anti-bullying coordinator who is trained to resolve bullying issues. If your school has a coordinator, ask him or her for help.

Typically, the anti-bullying policy contains both informal and formal complaint procedures. The policy will provide detailed instructions of who to contact in the school and how to complete the necessary paperwork to submit a complaint. The school must appropriately investigate and handle all complaints, as per school policy. In some cases, following an informal/formal procedure may be your best course of action to stop a bully, especially if you are seriously threatened or if you are subjected to physical violence.

If you need help or you are unsure if you should file a formal complaint, ask your parents for help. Your parents can contact the principal and work with you to complete the paperwork.

If you feel you can't safely identify yourself and fear retaliation, send an anonymous report to the principal. Provide a detailed description of what happened.

If your principal doesn't respond fast enough or ignores you, your parents can take your complaint to the superintendent or school board.

If the school offers you no help and you don't know whom to turn to, your parents can contact Lambda Legal [use their online email form to report the incident at www.LAMBDALEGAL.COM/ HELP]. *This is a serious step, so be sure to discuss with your parents to determine if this action is necessary.*

~Go to the Police for Cases of Severe Bullying~

In some cases bullying may be classified as a crime, which places it beyond the jurisdiction of schools. If you believe you are in danger of being physically hurt or the threats are extremely egregious, speak with your parents to help you file a report with your local police. There are extreme situations when contacting the police is the only way to stop a bully. If a bully leaves you no choice, contacting the police may be your best option.

~What To Do if You're Cyberbullied~

Prior to social media, it was easier to spot a bully. Typically they were the meanest, toughest, strongest or most obnoxious person in school. However, with the internet this is no longer the case. Now, a small weak child can be as much of a bully as someone who is big and strong, but with more impact. The only thing a person needs to possess is a bully mentality and the desire to bully someone.

Unlike traditional bullying, a cyberbully can be completely anonymous. Instead of bullying people face to face, bullies can hide behind the internet and bully people electronically. As a result, a cyberbully may represent the worst kind of bully. Technology and social media present many avenues a bully can use to harass someone including email, texting, Facebook, Twitter, Snapchat, Instagram, MySpace, etc. Now, not only words can hurt you, but pictures and images as well.

So, what can you do to stop a **Cyberbully**? Well, same as dealing with a bully encountered in person. There are actions you can take to stop it. Here are some actions to consider:

⁓*Use Block Feature/Change Privacy Settings*⁓

When someone is bullying you online, one of the best ways to stop it is to block and unfriend any account used to harass you. Social networking sites that require usernames allow users to block specific usernames or delete them from your buddy list and block any harassing accounts, email addresses, or phone numbers. As you know, you can always delete harassing or inappropriate messages, texts or posts; however, before you delete anything be sure to print a copy, which can be used later as evidence, if necessary.

Another way to stop online bullying is to change your privacy settings. Make sure that all your social media accounts have very strict privacy settings and set your accounts to "Friends Only" or "Private" for sites that have this feature. For Facebook, Twitter and other networking sites, you can adjust your settings so that only the people you select are able to see your personal information and posts.

On social networks, there are specific ways to stop or help prevent someone from bullying you.

Most network sites like Facebook and Twitter have "Safety Centers". These safety centers contain detailed information on how users can protect themselves against cyberbullies. For example, Facebook's safety center contains specific instruction on how to "unfriend" a person so that only your Facebook friends can contact you through Facebook Messenger chat or post on your timeline. There are instructions on how to "block" a person, that will prevent the person from adding you as a friend and viewing information you share on your timeline. Furthermore, Facebook describes how to report a person that is bullying you. Visit Facebook.com and Facebook Bullying Prevention Hub for more information.

In addition to Facebook and Twitter, there are other social network sites that provide instructions on how to protect you from online bullies. Instagram and Snapchat allow subscribers to "block" and "unfollow" users. YouTube allows users to flag videos that are deemed inappropriate. YouTube will determine whether the video breaks their terms of use. If it does, YouTube will remove it.

For more information regarding social media site security and to ensure procedures have not changed, contact the appropriate service provider. Cyberbullying violates the terms of service by social media sites, cell phone providers and other service providers. Read up on your service provider's policies and take the necessary steps to report threatening behavior.

~Don't Share Your Password~

Since computers have been around for many years, you might think people would know better and never share their password; however, studies show many people share their passwords with others. Your password is often the single key someone needs to gain access to your confidential information. In order to prevent someone from getting into your online account(s), make sure to keep your password a secret. Even if you think you can trust someone, they can intentionally or accidentally reveal your password to others, so don't share it. Statistics show that people who know your password often misuse it. Don't find out the hard way. You are the only person you can absolutely trust.

Follow this simple rule, **"Never share your password."**

~*Don't Use Social Media To Retaliate*~

When someone uses the internet to threaten or harass you, don't fall into the cyberbully's trap by responding to him or her with your own offensive message. Provoking a response from you is exactly what the cyberbully wants, so don't do it. Retaliation only further perpetuates the cycle of violence and does nothing to solve the problem. Instead, send a reply stating that you find the message offensive and politely say, "Please stop sending these types of messages." Always respond in a polite manner. If this doesn't work, reply stating, "If these types of offensive messages continue, I will escalate to a person of authority."

Lastly, never open messages from people you don't know, just delete them. The message might be from someone looking to bully you and the message could contain viruses and infect your computer.

~*Contact Law Enforcement*~

The same as with someone who bullies you in person, if the online threats are so severe or lead to physical violence, you may want to report them to your local police department. ***Before you contact the police, make sure to first discuss with your parents/guardian to determine if this action is appropriate.*** If the decision is to contact the police, be sure you take screenshots or save every email, text, picture, instant message, social media post and any other evidence of cyberbullying to support your complaint.

~~~IMPORTANT~~~

Don't ever feel the situation is completely hopeless or that there is nowhere to turn or no one to speak with. Just like traditional bullying, cyberbullying can be stopped. There is always something you can do to stop a bully, always some person who can help you. Just be sure to **"SAY SOMETHING—PLEASE, TELL SOMEONE."**

Remember: Never be bullied into silence.

For my final thought, I leave you with this quote from Chris Colfer—

"When people hurt you over and over, think of them like sandpaper. They may scratch and hurt you a bit, but in the end, you end up polished and they end up useless."

Wait, I can't believe it! I forgot to tell you something and it's huge.

Katie and I got married. This is the smartest thing I've ever done. We are happily married. I've come to realize one of the most important things in life is to simply be happy.

21

Final Bully Stories

There is a website (www.pacerteensagainstbullying.org/pacer-story/my-bullying-story-3/) where people of all ages can go to tell their story of how they were bullied. These are real stories as told by the people who have actually been bullied. This website provides an outlet where people can share information and help raise awareness of this growing problem. The next few pages contain some of the stories from people impacted by this horrible act called "bullying". The only changes made to the original stories posted were to correct grammatical errors.

My Bullying Story

November 18, 2015
Carolin

When I was in elementary school, I was a very happy and outgoing kid and had lots of friends. But when I started secondary school, some older kids started to bully and tease me. All my friends from elementary school left me because they didn't want to be seen with me. At my school, everything was all about money and clothes. I had huge glasses and I was really ugly and everyone laughed at me. Then a boy (he was in 8th grade I think) started to follow me around. He called me names, took my stuff and made up rumors about me. One day he and his friends beat me up on the bus. No one wanted to be friends with me anymore. Then I became friends with two girls in my class. They started making up rumors about me. Everyone kept telling me what a bad person I was.

In 6th grade, the bullying got even worse. Everyone said I was ugly and I should just kill myself. In 7th grade my mom made me attend afternoon classes (full-time school was voluntary at my school). The kids in afternoon class started bullying me, too. They followed me around and took photos of me in the bathroom and sent them to the whole school. When I got home from school, I would go to my room and cry all evening. I never talked to anyone. My grades dropped and my teachers started to talk to my parents. They told them I was lazy and refused to participate. They knew I was bullied but they never did anything to stop it. Everyone hated me and I didn't have a single friend. I just want to tell everyone who is going through the same: It gets better. I know it's really hard, and you might feel like giving up sometimes, but you have to be yourself and stay confident. Don't let them get to you. I know you're suffering, but at some point you'll be proud of yourself for all that you've been through. And if anyone judges you, it is their own problem. Those people have no idea what you've been through. They probably couldn't even take it. But you had to take it. And you're still here going on with your life. And that's why you can be proud of yourself.

Hope

November 27, 2018
Anonymous

I, too, was prey for the bullies that lurked the middle school halls, mostly verbal abuse, but even some physical. The verbal abuse consisted mostly of bashing my physical appearance and speaking about my parent's financial situation (we didn't have the most money, but we happily made do). It's something about the physical bullying that will always be engraved in my brain. I remember it like it happened yesterday. I was switching out books in my locker, which was on the bottom, when my top locker partner comes up behind me and starts violently kicking me and telling me to hurry. I just sat there and allowed him to kick me. I tried to laugh it off and open my lock as fast as possible to please him. Kids surrounding us were laughing. I didn't mention it until a few weeks later.

Luckily, I had a very caring 6th grade teacher who I will always remember. During those times, it was so easy to go along with the bullying crowd. I mean anything to get them off your back right? That is not what you should do. Remember kindness is always what you should strive for. The bullies will look back on those years of bullying and regret every second of it and feel shame and guilt for the awful things they've done, but you will remember that you kept composure, and most importantly, that you were kind. Please stay strong in this cruel world.

Prevention Is Part of the Cure

March 23, 2017
Anonymous

If you are being bullied please remember life is so short and life is what you make it, even when you feel like all hope is lost it really isn't! Don't hide your bullying like it's something to be ashamed of as you are not to blame, the bullies are! Find the inner strength and love for yourself that you would give in a heartbeat to someone you love as they do not deserve to lose you and the bullies do not deserve to win. Show them be it now or in time that you are the stronger person and your life means something.

213

To the bullies of the world, there must be someone you care about, a parent, a sibling, a friend or a child, you imagine someone making them feel insignificant, unwanted, afraid and alone. You may make excuses that you have suffered at the hands of bullies, maybe even by those who you loved and trusted, but if you are honest with yourself there really is no excuse, bullying shows weakness not power, regardless of life experiences.

I am a strong believer that you choose your own path and go one way or the other, why would you want to go down a similar path of destruction if that is what you have experienced? No one is worth impressing in pursuit of another person's misery, and the old 'sticks and stones' line is rubbish, words do hurt and do scar! Now is that really what you want to hold your legacy for in life? People really do save lives, if you are aware that bullying is taking place and don't do anything about it then you are just as much to blame. If you are a bully then stop and think, would I like someone to treat me this way? If you are being bullied then don't let them win. Remember, kindness costs nothing!

A Message to My 13 Year Old Self

May 22, 2017
Anonymous

This is not a bullying experience story. Rather, this is a bullying experience message. Writing was one of the things I did to let go and recover from my painful experience, thus I wrote this letter during the time I was struggling with painful memories. I'm sharing this with everyone because I want this letter to serve a purpose—and that is to send a message that no matter who you are, and no matter what you've been through or are going through, THERE IS HOPE and YOU ARE NOT ALONE.

Although some people make us view ourselves negatively, there is always something wonderful about us that we should be proud of. We should not be ashamed of ourselves. We should not listen to negative voices. We should keep in mind that although we are flawed… we are wonderful and perfect—just the way we are. We are enough.

To those of you who are being bullied, keep in mind that YOU HAVE A RIGHT TO BE RESPECTED—FIGHT FOR THAT RIGHT.

To those of you who have been bullied and whose wounds still haven't healed, remember that YOU WILL RECOVER—AND YOU WILL RISE UP AS A MUCH BETTER, WISER, AND STRONGER PERSON.

You are fearfully and wonderfully made. Greatly blessed and deeply loved. You can use your experience to make a big change, to serve a purpose.

Stay strong, better days are coming!

~Important Announcement: Kindness is never overrated.~

End Notes

[Note: If you have trouble accessing the links provided, conduct an online search using all text and include the link in your search]

Chapter 16 – Cyberbullying

171 APECSEC Admin, Advantages and Disadvantages of Social Networking, <http://www.APECSEC.ORG/advantages-and-disadvantages-of-social-networking/> [May 18,2014]

171 Charlie R. Claywell, Advantages and Disadvantages of Social Networking – Love to Know, <http://socialnetworking.lovetoknow.com/advantages_and_disadvantages_of_social_networking>

171 Cyberbullying Research Center, Cyberbullying Stories, <http://www.cyberbullying.org/resources>

Chapter 17 – What is Bullying

183 Wikipedia (Search on-line "What is bullying")

Chapter 18 – Bully Statistics

187 Stephan Merrill, Anatomy of School Bullying, Understanding the Hot Spots Within School is Essential to Putting a Stop to Student Bullying, <http://www.edutopia.com> [March 21, 2017]

188 Traditional Bullying, <http://www.meganmeierfoundation.org/bullying/>

188 Bully Statistics & Information, <http://www.americanspcc.org/bullying/statitics-and-information>

188 John M Grohol, Psy.D, Facts & Statistics on Bullying, LIB, <http://www.psychcentral.com/lib/facts-statistics-on-bullying> [May 24, 2016]

Chapter 19 – Why Do People Bully

192 10 Causes of Bullying, <http://www.americanspcc.org/bullying-and-schools>

192 What Does A Bully Get Out Of Bullying People, <http://www.7cups.com/qa-bullying-10/what-does-a-bully-get-out-of-bullying-people-485/> [Passionate Music, February 24, 2016 5:56AM]

192 Farouk M Radwan MSc., Reasons Why People Bully Others, <http://www.2knowmyself.com/reasons_why_people_bully_others>

192 Rachael Rettner, Bullies on Bullies: Why We Do It, <https://www.livescience.com/11163-bullies-bullying.html> [August 26, 2010]

193 Causes of Bullying, Bullies Are Often Jealous of or Frustrated with the Person They are Bullying, <http://www.americanspcc. org/ wp-content/uploads/2013/04/bullying-causes-of-courtesy-of-nobullying.pdf> (Courtesy of nobullying.org)

193 Samuel Ha, Why Do People Bully? 9 Reasons People Bully, <http://mightyfighter.com/why-do-people-bully>

193 Dealing with Bullies, Why Do Bullies Act That Way, <http:// www.kidshealth.org/en/kids/bullies.html>

193 Some Reasons Why Someone May Bully, <http://www. befrienders.org/reasons-for-bullying/>

193 Most High School Bullies Are Sociopaths Who Seek Power, <https://www.reddit.com/r/changemyview/comments/6wf4le/ cmv_most_high_school_bullies_are_sociopaths_who/>

193 What is Bullying, <http://www.stopbullying.gov/what-is-bullying/index.html>

194 T. M. Gaouette, 10 Things Bullies Don't Want You to Know, <http://www.projectinspired.com/10-things-bullies-don't-want-you-to-know/> [November 26, 2013]

194 Causes of Bullying, Looking for Attention, <http://www. americanspcc.org/wp-content/uploads/2013/04/bullying-causes-of-courtesy-of-nobullying.pdf> (Courtesy of nobullying. org)

195 Causes of Bullying, Bullies Come From Dysfunctional Families, <http://www.americanspcc.org/wp-content/uploads/2013/04/ bullying-causes-of-courtesy-of-nobullying.pdf> (Courtesy of nobullying.org)

195 Causes of Bullying, Someone Else is Bullying Them, <http://www.americanspcc.org/wp-content/uploads/2013/04/bullying-causes-of-courtesy-of-nobullying.pdf> (Courtesy of nobullying.org)

195 Bullying Statistics, Why Do People Bully, Family Issues, <http://www.bullyingstatistics.org/content/why-do-people-bully.html>

Chapter 20 – What To Do When Bullied

200 How To Deal With Abusive Street Teens, Preventing Negative Interactions, Travel In Groups of Two or More, <http://www.wikihow.com/deal-with-abusive-street-teens>

200 How To Avoid Being Bullied in Middle School, Deterring Bullies, Avoid Bullies Altogether, <http://www.wikihow.com/avoid-being-bullied-in-middle-school>

200 5 Skills You Need To Teach Your Kids When Handling Bullies, Avoid Isolation, <http://www.sg.theasianparent.com/how-should-kids-handle-bullies>

200 Sherri Gordon, 9 Self-Defense Strategies to Ward Off Bullying, Stay in a Group, <http://www.verywellfamily.com/how-kids-can-defend-themselves-against-bullies-460789> [February 14, 2018]

201 How To Stop Being Bullied, Handling a Bully, Don't React With More Bullying, <http://www.wikihow.com/stop-being-bullied>

201 What To Do If You're Bullied, <http://www.stopbullying.gov/kids/what-you-can-do/index.html>

201 Dawson's Blog, What To Do If You Are being Bullied, Don't Fight Back, <http://www.thehopeline.com/if-you-are-being-bullied>

202 Dealing with Bullies, If The Bully Says or Does Something to You, <http://www.kidshealth.org/en/kids/bullies.html>

202 How To Avoid Being Bullied in Middle School, Deterring Bullies, Hang Out in Groups, <http://www.wikihow.com/avoid-being-bullied-in-middle-school>

202 <http://www.sample-registration-letters.com>

203 Example of an Anti Bullying Policy, <http://www.bullypolice.org/bullying_policy.PDF>

204 Youth What To Do If Bullied, <http://www.lambdalegal.org/know-your-rights/article/youth-what-to-do-if-bullied>

205 Dealing With Cyberbullying, <http://www.seventeen.com/life/a14724/dealing-with-cyberbullying>

205 Scott Meech, Cyberbullying: Worse Than Traditional Bullying, Educator's eZine, <http://www.techlearning.com/news/cyber-bullying-worse-than-traditional-bullying> [2007]

205 Digital Threat: The Impact of Cyberbullying, <http://www.tuw.edu/content/health/impact-of-cyberbullying>

205 <http://www.pacer.org/bullying/resources/cyberbullying> (click link Kowalski, Giumetti, Schroeder, & Lattanner, 2014)

205 Prevent Cyberbullying & Internet Harassment, What to Do If You're Bullied, <http://www.cyberbully411.com/what-to-do>

206 Bullying on Social Media, What Can I Do If I'm Being Bullied On Line, <http://www.plannedparenthood.org/learn/teens/bullying-safety-privacy/bullying/bullying-social-media>

206 What Can You Do To Help Prevent Cyberbullying, <http://www.endcyberbullying.net/preventing-cyberbullying>

206 Facebook Safety Center, <http://www.facebook.com/safety>

206 Twitter Safety Center, <https://about.twitter.com/en_us/safety/safety-tools.html>

206 Instagram Safety Center, <http://www.wellbeing.instagram.com/safety>

206 Snapchat Safety Center, <http://www.snap.com/en-US/safety/safety-center>

206 YouTube Safety Center, <http://youtube/yt/about/policies/#staying-safe>

207 Per Christensson, Don't Share Your Password (With Anyone), <http:/pc.net/tips/2014-03/dont_share_your_password> [March 2014]

207 Preventing Cyberbullying, Keep Your Password a Complete Secret, <http://www.wikihow.com/avoid-being-bullied-in-middle-school#preventing-cyber-bullying>

208 TipsToHelpStopCyberbullying, Don't Respond or Retaliate, <http://www.connectsafely.org/tips-to-help-stop-cyberbullying/> [May 7, 2018]

208 Brooke De Lench, 10 Tips for Teens to Prevent Cyberbullying, <http://www.momsteam.com/health-safety/10-tips-teens-prevent-cyberbullying>

208 Sameer Hinduja, PH.D and Justin W. Patchin, PH.D, Responding to Cyberbullying [Top Ten Tips for Teens], <http://www.cyberbullying.org/responding-to-cyberbullying-top-ten-tips-for-teens> January 2012)

208 Bullying and Cyberbullying, Tips For Dealing With Cyberbullying, <http://www.helpguide.org/articles/abuse/bullying-and-cyberbullying.htm>

208 Branter's Top Tips For Responding To Cyberbullying, Never Retaliate, <http://www.sd27j.org/cms/lib/co01900701/centricity/domain/8/cyberbullying%20flyer.pdf> [Fall 2017]

Chapter 21 – Final Bully Stories

210 Real Life – Final Bully Stories <www.pacerteensagainstbullying.org/pacer-story/my-bullying-story-3/>

Author's Request – Message to Readers

First and foremost, I want to thank you for reading School and My Bully Experience. I hope you enjoyed reading the book as much as I enjoyed writing it.

Can you do me a big favor and write a **Book Review**? It's fast and easy. Just access Amazon at www.amazon.com. In the search field, enter "School and My Bully Experience." When School and My Bully Experience appears on the screen, click on the total number of reviews located next to the five (5) stars. **Finally**, click on the **"Write a Review"** link, enter your review and click **"Submit."**

That's it. You're done.

Your review will provide valuable information to potential readers.

Your time and effort is greatly appreciated.

Many thanks – Frank Joseph Minichetti

Important: You must have an account with Amazon in order to leave a review. If you do not have an account, your parent/guardian may have one, please ask them for permission/assistance if you want to leave a review.

About the Author

Frank Joseph Minichetti is a passionate reader and writer. He spent most of his career in the field of Information and Technology. Although throughout his career he wrote technical documentation and content for various websites, he finally fulfilled his life-long dream of writing a book.

Currently, he works as a substitute teacher, enjoying his interactions with students. His favorite subject is Language Arts, of course. When not substitute teaching, he spends most of his free time writing.

When suffering from writer's block, he can be found at the  Jersey shore, sitting on the beach, gazing at the ocean for inspiration. One of his favorite things to do – dog sit for his daughter's toy poodle, Peanut.

Mr. Minichetti has a daughter (Kris Ann) and a son-in-law (Peter) and lives with his wife Betty in Bergen County, New Jersey.

Author Website: https://frankjosephminichetti.com
Email: frank@frankjosephminichetti.com